Dawn and the Impossible Three

Join the Club!

Be part of something special!

The Babysitters Club

The Summer Before

Kristy's Great Idea

Claudia and the Phantom
Phone Calls

The Truth About Stacey

Mary Anne Saves the Day

Be part of something special!

The Babysitters Club

Dawn and the Impossible Three

Ann M. Martin

SCHOLASTIC

Scholastic Children's Books
An imprint of Scholastic Ltd
Euston House, 24 Eversholt Street
London, NW1 1DB, UK
Registered office: Westfield Road, Southam, Warwickshire, CV47 0RA
SCHOLASTIC and associated logos are trademarks and/or registered
trademarks of Scholastic Inc.

First published in the US by Scholastic Ltd, 1987
First published in the UK by Scholastic Inc, 1990

This edition published in the UK by Scholastic Ltd, 2011

ISBN 978 1407 12046 1

Printed in the UK by CPI Bookmarque, Croydon, Surrey.
Papers used by Scholastic Children's Books are made from
wood grown in sustainable forests.

1 3 5 7 9 10 8 6 4 2

www.scholastic.co.uk/zone

For Aunt Dot

Chapter 1

The Babysitters Club. I didn't start it and I don't run it, but I am its newest member. I'm Dawn Schafer, babysitter number five. The other girls in the club have titles, like Mary Anne Spier, secretary, or Claudia Kishi, vice president. But I'm just me.

The club is the most important thing in my life. If it weren't for the club, I wouldn't be riding my bicycle off to another babysitting job at this very moment. And if it weren't for all the babysitting jobs I've had, I wouldn't know so many people here in Stoneybrook.

See, I've only lived in Connecticut a few months. Until this past January, I lived in California with my parents and my younger brother, Jeff. But last autumn Mom and Dad split up, and Mom decided to move back to the place where she grew up. Her parents still live here. So right after Christmas, Jeff and I were uprooted from hot, sunny California and transplanted to cold, sloppy Connecticut, where (so far) it's never been warm enough for me.

I hate cold weather. On the days when the temperature slips back a few degrees, I yell at the weatherman. On the days when it creeps up, I congratulate him and apologize for yelling. I'm still not sure what the big deal about New England winters is all about. Back in California, we had one season: summer. I thought it was wonderful. I loved the beach, I loved sunshine, I loved thirty-degree Christmases. Why, I wondered, would anyone want to interrupt all that warmth with three other seasons?

The family I was babysitting for that afternoon was the Pikes. There are eight Pike children – and three of them are triplets! However, I wasn't going to sit for all of them. The triplets, who are nine-year-old boys, would be at ice hockey practice (my brother Jeff was there, too), and eight-year-old Vanessa would be at her violin lesson. That left Nicky, who's seven; Margo (six); Claire (four); and Mallory, who's ten and usually a big help.

When I reached the Pikes', I parked my bicycle at the side of the drive and rang the doorbell.

"I'll get it! I'll get it!" cried a voice from inside.

The door was flung open by Claire, the

youngest Pike. She loves answering the door and the phone.

"Hi, Claire!" I said brightly.

Claire suddenly turned shy. She put her finger in her mouth and looked at the floor. "Hi," she replied.

"I'm Dawn. Remember me?"

Claire nodded.

"Can I come in?"

She nodded again.

As I was opening the door, Mrs Pike ran down the stairs. "Oh, it's you, Dawn. Terrific! You're right on time. How are you?"

"Fine, thanks," I answered.

I really like Mrs Pike. She has lots of energy and she loves kids. (She'd have to, I guess.) She's patient and funny and hardly ever yells. She and Mr Pike have been really nice to our family ever since we moved here.

"I'm just going to be at a meeting of the trustees of the public library. The library number is on the message board by the phone. If you need to call me, ask for the Prescott Room and say that I'm in the board meeting, OK?"

"OK."

(Mrs Pike is always so organized. She's a babysitter's dream.)

3

"The emergency numbers are in their usual spot, and the kids can have a snack – a small one – if they're hungry. I'll be home a little after five. Is that all right?"

"Perfect. We have a Babysitters Club meeting at five-thirty."

Our club is run very professionally. We meet three times a week to go over club business and take job calls. (We get tons of jobs.) The president is Kristy Thomas. She's the one who had the idea for the club.

The vice president is Claudia Kishi, who's really neat and sophisticated. She lives across the street from Kristy. We hold our meetings in Claudia's room because she has a phone. Claudia is Japanese and beautiful. She hates school, but loves art and mystery stories. She's a little bit hard to get to know.

The club treasurer is Stacey McGill. Stacey moved to Stoneybrook just a few months before I did, so we have something in common. She came from New York City, and I know she had trouble getting adjusted to small-town life. Sometimes we talk about that.

Then there's Mary Anne Spier. She's the one who introduced me to Kristy, Claudia and Stacey. She's the secretary of the club and responsible for the Babysitters Club Record Book, which is where she records our job appointments, as well as the phone numbers and addresses of our clients and stuff like that. (Also in that book is a record of the money we earn. Stacey's in charge of that section.)

We keep a Babysitters Club Notebook, too, which is like a diary. Kristy insists that we write up *each* job we take and that we all read the book every few days. That's so we know what's going on in the families the club sits for.

The most important thing about Mary Anne (to me, anyway) is that she's my new best friend. (My old best friend was Sunny Winslow in California.) Mary Anne lives next door to Kristy Thomas, and for the longest time Kristy was her only best friend. Now I'm Mary Anne's other best friend.

The wildest thing happened right after Mary Anne and I got to know each other. It turned out that her father and my mother went to high school together. Not only *that*, they dated – for a long time. They were really serious about each other. Mary Anne and I found all this romantic stuff they'd written to each other in their senior yearbooks.

Even more amazing is that they've started dating each other *again*! (Mary Anne's mother died when Mary Anne was really little.) Mary Anne and I can hardly believe that our parents are going out. It's so exciting! Mr Spier is this stern, lonely guy who needs some fun in his life (and something to think about besides Mary Anne, who's his only kid). And my mom has been so sad since the divorce. She needs some fun, too.

Mrs Pike was putting on her coat and hat and tossing things in her purse. "Mallory's upstairs doing her homework," she told me, "but she'll be down soon. She wants to see you. Margo's in the playroom, and Nicky's at the Barretts' playing with Buddy. Do you know the Barretts?"

I shook my head.

"They live a few doors down – towards your house. Our kids and their kids are back and forth all the time. Nicky'll probably bring Buddy over here at some point today. You won't need to call Mrs Barrett. She's very relaxed, and she'll probably know he's here anyway."

"OK," I said.

"I guess that's it." Mrs Pike stooped down to kiss Claire. "See you later, pumpkin," she said. "Wear your jacket if you go outside. It's chilly today." (Was it ever!) Then she called upstairs to Mallory and downstairs to Margo to let them know she was leaving – and she was gone.

I looked at Claire. "Let's go see what Margo's doing, OK?"

Claire nodded and I led her down to the playroom.

What Margo was doing was performing. She had put on a big floppy straw hat and a long filmy dress with some beads and scarves, and was dancing around to "Puff, the Magic Dragon", which was playing at full volume. When she knew the words, she mouthed them.

Claire and I plopped ourselves down on the couch and pretended we were the audience. When the song ended, Margo made a sweeping bow and Claire and I clapped loudly.

"Bravo!" I shouted.

"Diavo!" Claire shouted.

Margo took another bow.

I heard a clatter of footsteps in the kitchen and Mallory called down, "Hi, Dawn. What's eight times seven?"

"Hi, Mal," I called back. "You know that one."

"Fifty-six?" she asked.

"Right!" I said.

"Thanks!"

She returned to her homework.

Margo put "Old MacDonald Had a Farm" on and began another performance. Claire joined in on the animal sounds. They were just finishing when I heard Mallory in the kitchen again.

"Homework's done," she announced. "Can I have a snack, Dawn?"

"Sure," I replied. "Claire and Margo and I will have one, too."

The four of us sat around the Pikes' kitchen, eating granola bars.

"So, Dawn," said Mallory, "how's your new-old house?"

Claire and Margo giggled. Mallory had christened our house "new-old," and the little girls think it's funny, but Mallory's right. I do live in a new-old house. It's new to Mom and Jeff and me, but it was built in 1795. I love it, even though it's dark inside, and the stairway is narrow, and the doorways are low because people were a lot shorter in 1795. I like to think that I live in a house that so many other people have lived in – people who saw the War of 1812 and the Civil War and the Emancipation Proclamation and the first airplane and the Depression and the first rocket ship. It's exciting.

I bet our house has a secret passageway somewhere. Maybe it was even part of the Underground Railroad. Mary Anne and I are going to explore it thoroughly one day. We'll tap on walls and press the wood panelling, hoping for something to spring out or swing open. We plan to explore the attic, too. Maybe we'll find an old diary or something.

I smiled to myself, thinking that Mom would want to be in on a search of the house. She loves things like that. She thinks they're romantic, and Mom is a very romantic person. That's one reason Mr Spier liked her so much when they were in high school. Guess what she did? She saved the rose tied with a white ribbon that he gave her the night of their senior prom. She pressed it between the pages of her yearbook. It's still there. Mary Anne and I found it.

"The new-old house is fine," I replied.

Mallory grinned at me and raised her eyebrows. "And how's your *mom*?" she asked meaningfully. Mallory knows about my mother and Mr Spier, and loves to hear about them. She likes most of all to hear about when they were in love in high school and what had happened to drive them apart. I'd told her as much as I knew, which wasn't much. Several times I had asked Mom why she and Mary Anne's father ended their relationship. It had something to do with Mom's parents not approving of the Spiers because they didn't have much money (Mom's parents have *tons* of money), but I didn't know the whole story.

"Honey," she'd said, "it's not really very interesting."

"I think it is. You two were in love, but you went off to college and never saw each other again. I think it's romantic . . . and sad."

"Our paths just never crossed. Our vacations usually came at different times. During the summers, I stayed in California and worked. And at Christmas time, Granny and Pop-Pop would take me to the Bahamas."

"Didn't you think about Mr Spier, though?"

"Sometimes, yes. But we were young. We had new lives and new interests. We were both busy with school. And then I met your father, and Mr Spier met Mary Anne's mother – and you know the rest of the story."

I sure did. The rest of the story is that my mother and father got married, got unhappy, and got divorced. They just weren't right for each other. Dad is super-organized. And Mom is a crazy person – not nasty crazy, just an absent-minded-professor type.

Jeff and I are actually *used* to finding the mixing bowls carefully put away in the linen closet, or finding her mending clothes we outgrew two years earlier. And although we've been living in our new-old house for several months, there is still a gigantic pile of unpacked cartons in the dining room. Every now and then I start to go through one, and each time Mom runs in and says, "Dawn, you don't have to bother with that, honey. Let me do it." And then she doesn't do it.

My mom is really terrific, but her habits are what drove her and Dad apart. I'm not saying the divorce was her fault. I'm just saying that she's disorganized and Dad couldn't live with that.

I didn't tell Mallory all that, though. What I said was, "Mom's OK. She's still going out with Mr Spier."

"Yay!" cried Mallory.

"And she's started looking for a job. She's always off on interviews—"

We were interrupted by a thump and a wail that seemed to come from the front porch. Mallory and I looked at each other. "What was that?" I asked.

We raced to the door. There was Nicky Pike with a boy about his age, and a round-faced, pigtailed little girl who was crying.

"Suzi!" Mallory exclaimed. "It's Suzi Barrett," she informed me. "And this is Buddy, her brother."

"She fell coming up the steps," Buddy said. "I think she skinned her knee."

I braved the cold weather to dart outside and roll up Suzi's trouser legs. Sure enough, one knee was bleeding, but it didn't look bad. "I'm Dawn, Suzi," I told her. "Why don't you come in and I'll wash your cut and find you a plaster."

"Thanks," said Suzi tearfully.

"We have plasters with dinosaurs on them," Nicky said helpfully.

We found one and I put it carefully over Suzi's scrape. She liked it so much that she rolled up the leg of her trousers and left it that way so everyone could see the plaster.

Suzi and Buddy stayed at the Pikes' the rest of the afternoon. Suzi watched *Sesame Street* with Claire and Margo, and Mallory helped Nicky and Buddy make a dinosaur village. (I never did figure out what that was.)

When Mrs Pike got home, it was five-fifteen and time to make tracks to the Babysitters Club meeting. I said goodbye to the children, got on my bike and rode off in a hurry, deciding to go to Mary Anne's house and pick her up beforehand.

When I reached the Spiers', I guided my bicycle into the drive and pulled to a stop. While I was fiddling with the kickstand, Mary Anne burst through her front door and dashed across the lawn.

"Hey, guess what!" she cried. "Great news!"

Chapter 2

Mary Anne's brown hair flew behind her as she ran to me.

"What? What is it?" I asked excitedly.

"Dad just called. He said not to expect him for dinner tonight."

"So?" I prompted.

"He said not to expect him because he's taking your mom out!"

"Another date!" I squealed. "Fantastic! This is really exciting."

Mary Anne closed her eyes and sighed. "Yeah. The date was spur-of-the-moment, too, which is a good sign. Dad never used to just haul off and do things. He'd plan them for weeks. But he said he got the idea about five minutes ago, called your mother, asked her to join him for a quick dinner, and then called me. I can't believe it."

I checked my watch. "It's almost five-thirty," I said. "We'd better get to Claudia's."

Mary Anne started across the street with me, but she didn't say anything, just sighed again. It was a sigh of pleasure.

I knew one reason Mary Anne was so happy about her father and my mother. It was because my mother took Mr Spier's mind off Mary Anne. Mr Spier used to make all these rules for Mary Anne: she had to fix her hair in plaits and wear the clothes he bought for her; she couldn't talk on the phone after dinner; she had to be in by nine; she had to put half of her babysitting money in the bank; etc. etc. It was awful.

He was already beginning to change when he "re-met" Mom, but now he's a completely different father. He let Mary Anne get contact lenses to replace her reading glasses. He allows her to spend her babysitting money if she saves her allowance, and since he no longer buys her clothes, you should see what Mary Anne gets with her money. She doesn't look like Claudia or Stacey, who wear these really wild outfits such as tight black trousers and Day-Glo shirts, but, well, for instance, at that very moment as we walked across the Kishis' lawn, Mary Anne had on her first sweatshirt and her first pair of jeans ever. She looked terrific!

"You know what I'm going to start doing?"

Mary Anne asked me with a giant grin.

"What?"

"Redecorating my room."

"No! Really?"

"Really. I used to think that the only way I'd be able to redecorate was if my father lost his mind. I guess he did lose it – over your mother."

"Thanks a lot!" I said.

"Oh, you know what I mean. I think it's great."

"Great that he and Mom are going out, or great that he's lost his mind?"

Mary Anne giggled. "Both," she said.

"What are you going to do to your room?"

"I'm going to take all the babyish stuff off my walls and put up posters and photographs. That's all I can afford to do. Then I'll have to work on my dad a little. I have to see if he'll help me do anything expensive. I want a new bedspread and a new rug and new curtains and new wallpaper. Every-thing in my room is pink, and I can't stand pink!"

We reached the Kishis' front stoop. I rang the bell.

Claudia's sister Janine answered the door.

Mary Anne and I glanced at each other. Janine is fifteen years old. She's a genius. Mary

Anne and Kristy don't like her because she's so smart, and she's always correcting whatever they say. But I don't mind Janine. I think she's all right. You just have to know how to handle her.

"Hi, Janine!" I said.

Mary Anne hung back. She's shy around some people.

"Hi," Janine answered. "I suppose you're here for a meeting of your club."

"Yup," I said.

"You know," Janine began, "the expression 'yup'—"

"Janine," I interrupted her, "did you notice Mary Anne's clothes? She has new jeans and a new sweatshirt. She bought them with her own money – money she earned babysitting."

"The club must be doing awfully well," Janine commented.

"Oh, it is. Extremely well." I decided to toss out a few big words. "Thanks to the foresight of our president, it's both profitable and proficient . . . profusely proficient," I added. "Well, we must continue on."

We ran past Janine and up the stairs, but I could hear Janine yell after us, " 'Continue on' is redundant!"

I didn't know what *redundant* meant, and I didn't care.

We entered Claudia's room. Claudia was sitting cross-legged on her bed while her grandmother, Mimi, brushed her hair. Claudia's hair is absolutely beautiful. It's long and jet-black and always shiny. She uses special stuff in it.

Claudia and Stacey have suddenly taken great interest in their hair. One night a week they muck it up with an egg rinse. On Wednesdays and Sundays they squeeze lemon juice on it – from real lemons. They keep telling me I should use eggs and lemons in my hair, too. I have long, l-o-n-g hair (almost down to my bottom). It's thin and fine, and so blonde it's white. Mom says it's like corn silk. Claudia says the egg would give it body. Stacey says the lemon would make it shiny. I say it's my hair and what I do with it is my business. (I plan to try an avocado paste on it. If Claudia and Stacey and I put our heads together, we'd have a salad.)

"Hello, girls," Mimi greeted us in her gentle accent. "Is it time for your meeting?"

"Yes," Mary Anne replied, leaning over to kiss Mimi on the cheek. She and Mimi are special friends.

"Well, then, I will leave you to your work."

Mimi rose and left the room, just as Stacey thundered up the stairs. She was followed a few moments later by Kristy.

"Hi, everybody!" called Kristy. "We're all here! Great. It's fee collection day. Did you guys bring your money? Did you bring the treasury, Stacey?"

Kristy never wastes a second. She's a take-charge, rushing-around kind of person. Sometimes she's bossy, but not too often. Mary Anne says she used to be a lot worse, but now she tries to watch herself.

"Here's the treasury," said Stacey. She dumped the contents of the treasury (a manila envelope) on to the bed. Several dollar bills and a whole mess of quarters fell out. "Seven-fifty," she said, after counting the money quickly.

We each kicked in our weekly fees.

"Not bad," said Kristy. "Maybe we should buy some stuff for the Kid-Kits."

Kid-Kits are boxes that we Babysitters sometimes bring along on jobs. Mostly they're filled with our old games and toys and picture books (which are new to the kids we sit for), but we also keep them stocked with colouring books, sticker books, puzzle books, and other stuff that we have to replace from time to time. We pay for

18

those things out of club fees. The stuff we buy is worth it. Kids love our Kid-Kits, so they ask their parents to use the Babysitters Club and we end up getting more jobs. My dad always used to say, "You have to spend money to make money." He's a good businessman. And I guess Kristy is a good businesswoman.

Ring, ring.

Our first phone call. Claudia answered it.

"Hello. Babysitters Club. . . Oh, hi. . . Saturday, from three to five? I'll check around and call you right back. Bye." She hung up the phone.

Mary Anne had already opened the record book to the calendar section. "This Saturday?" she asked.

"Nope, the next one," replied Claudia. "That was Mrs Prezzioso. She needs someone for Jenny for two hours that afternoon. Who's free then?"

The Babysitters Club rule for calls that come in during meetings is that every member has a chance at each job. If someone calls one of us at home some other time, that's a different story. We can take those jobs on the spot, of course. But club calls are for the group.

Mary Anne checked the calendar. "We're all free then," she said.

"Well, don't worry about me," said Claudia

quickly. "I – I think I might have to go shopping that day."

"Yeah, me, too," said Stacey. "With Claudia." You could tell that the idea had just occurred to them.

"And I think that . . . that I promised David Michael I'd take him to the new Disney movie then," Kristy said in a rush. David Michael is Kristy's little brother. (She also has two big brothers in high school.) As far as I know, she has never taken David Michael to a movie.

Mary Anne looked at me.

"You take the job," I said grandly.

The truth is, nobody really likes Jenny Prezzioso except Mary Anne. The rest of us think Jenny is a spoiled brat. And that her parents are weird. But Mary Anne handles the Prezziosos well, and for some reason she kind of likes Jenny.

Claudia called Mrs P. back to tell her who would be sitting, and Mary Anne noted the job in the record book. Two more calls came in. The first was from Mrs Newton, needing a sitter for four-year-old Jamie (one of our all-time favourite little kids), and the other was from Watson Brewer.

Mr Brewer was calling so far in advance that once again all five of us were free, but we very generously gave the job to Kristy. That's because

Mr Brewer (Kristy and the other girls call him Watson) is going to become Kristy's stepfather this fall!

Kristy's parents got divorced a few years ago, and sometime last year Mrs Thomas started seeing this really rich man, Watson Brewer, who lives in a mansion (no kidding, a real mansion) across town. Mr Brewer is also divorced. He has two little kids, Karen and Andrew. Mostly they live with their mother, but every other weekend and on certain holidays, they stay with Mr Brewer. Kristy really loves those kids, and since she's about to become their stepsister, we always let her take Mr Brewer's jobs if she's free.

Ring, ring.

This time I answered the phone. "Good afternoon. Babysitters Club."

"Hello?" said an uncertain voice on the other end of the line.

"Hello?" I said again.

"Hello, I – Mrs Pike gave me your number. I need a babysitter. Actually, I'm going to be needing a lot of sitters. And your organization was very highly recommended. I live over on Slate Street, just down from the Pikes."

"Well," I said briskly. "Thank you very much. May I ask you some questions?" Kristy and the other club members had trained me on handling new clients.

"Never take them on without finding out certain important information first," Kristy had told me.

"How many children do you have?" I asked.

"Three," she replied. "Buddy, my oldest, is seven. He's Hamilton, Junior, actually. Suzi is four, and Marnie is the baby. She's a year and a half."

"Buddy and Suzi?" I said. "Is this Mrs Barrett?"

"Why, yes, it is."

"I met Buddy and Suzi over at the Pikes' today." I told her about Suzi's knee. Then I asked a few more questions, and after that Mrs Barrett said nervously, "I guess you should know that my husband and I have just divorced. This is a hard time for my children. I've got to find a job and they're used to having their father around, and I'm not a terribly organized person."

Wow. I could sympathize with that.

When it turned out that I was the only one available on the afternoon Mrs Barrett needed a sitter, I was secretly glad. I barely knew her kids, and already I felt close to them.

Chapter 3

"Hi, I'm home!"

"Honey, I'm leaving!"

I got back to my house that evening just as Mom was on her way out to meet Mr Spier for dinner.

She kissed my forehead and ducked under the low doorway. "I should be back in a couple of hours," she told me from the front porch.

"OK," I said. "Have fun." I started to close the door. We were letting cold air in.

"Dinner's ready for you and Jeff."

"OK." I started to close the door again. I was freezing.

"It's in the double boiler on the stove."

"OK—"

"And there's salad in the fridge."

"OK." Just when it looked like I really might be able to close the door, I suddenly had to open it wide. "Mom, come back here," I said.

She ducked back inside. "What?"

"Look," I said, pointing. "Only one earring, a rubber band around your wrist, and a price tag on your skirt. Mom, for heaven's sake."

Mom laughed sheepishly. "What would I do without you, Dawn?" She pulled off the rubber band, removed the price tag, and started out the door.

"Earring!" I yelled.

"Oh, *darn!*" exclaimed Mom. "I don't know where the other one is. Does this one look too funny by itself?"

"Well, it looks sort of punk."

"Punk!" Mom spit the word out as if it tasted bad. She yanked off the earring and handed it to me. "I'll do without earrings," she said. "You and Jeff behave yourselves. I'll be back soon."

"Say hi to Mr Spier for me," I called.

"I will!" Mom dashed off, waving over her shoulder, and climbed into her car.

I closed the front door and stood around in the hall with my jacket on, trying to warm up. Then I walked through the living room and collected the things that didn't belong there: a can of hair spray, a bicycle pump, a jar of instant coffee and a ladle. Sometimes I thought our entire house (except for my room) was like one big game of What's Wrong with This Picture?

I put the hair spray, the pump, the coffee, the ladle and Mom's earring away. In our dark little kitchen, I lifted the lid on the double boiler and peeked inside. I sniffed. I poked at the stuff with a fork.

"Hey, Jeff—" I started to shout.

"It's Leftover Stew," he called from the den, before I had even asked the question.

Oh, gross. Ew, ew, ew. Leftover Stew.

I checked our freezer. "Hey, Jeff!" I shouted again.

"There's all-natural frozen meatless pizza," he replied. "Couldn't we have that?"

"Definitely." I popped the frozen pizza in the oven. Then I wandered into the den.

My brother was sprawled on the sofa, watching a cartoon show. "What're you going to do with the stew?" he asked.

"Put it back in the fridge. Maybe Mom will eat it."

"I wish we had a dog," Jeff said. "Dogs love leftovers." Jeff's eyes never left the TV screen.

I returned to the kitchen and checked the pizza. Then I sat down at the table and tried to begin my homework, but I couldn't concentrate. I got up and walked slowly through our house.

I didn't care that it was dark or that the rooms

were small or that everything was low down. I thought it was cosy. I was glad, however, that the kitchen and the bathrooms had been remodelled. Actually, I was glad to have bathrooms at all. The old outhouse was still in our back garden, at the edge of the property. I had looked in it once. Yick. Dark, dusty, and full of cobwebs. A Colonial kitchen might have been fun – but not very practical. I wondered how long it would take to bake a pizza in a fireplace.

Ding! The oven timer went off.

"Hey, Jeff, it's pizza!" I yelled.

Jeff dragged himself away from the TV while I went back to the kitchen. I returned the Leftover Stew to the refrigerator. Jeff got out plates, napkins, forks and the salad.

We sat down across from each other. I was starving.

No sooner had I lifted a piece of steaming, spicy, melty pizza to my mouth than the phone rang.

I looked at Jeff. He was faster than I. He'd already had the pizza *in* his mouth. He looked at me.

"Would you puh-*lease* get the phone?" I pleaded. The pizza smelled so good it was making me dizzy.

"Mphhhyrst?" Jeff asked. He'd taken the biggest bite in the history of the world.

"Never mind." With a gigantic sigh I put the pizza back on my plate. I answered the phone on the fourth ring.

"Hi, it's me," said Mary Anne's voice. "What are you doing?"

"Eating dinner," I replied. My mouth was watering.

"Oh. I just ate. I had a sandwich. What are you eating?"

"Pizza. Hey, I should have asked you over so you wouldn't have to eat alone."

"That's OK. Maybe next time. Listen, I had a great idea. Do you want to help me redo my room?"

"Sure! That would be fun. Hey! You know what?"

"What?" asked Mary Anne.

"We've got some stuff I bet you could use. Our house in California was bigger than this one, and we've got cartons of things up in the attic that we don't have room for. I know there are a few posters somewhere. And there's this neat reading lamp that used to be in my room. And probably some pillows, too."

"Doesn't your mom want those things?" asked

27

Mary Anne, sounding worried. Honestly, she's the biggest worrier.

"Nah. We were going to have a garage sale, but Mom realized there wasn't really enough stuff for a sale, and then she couldn't decide what to do with it, so she piled it into the downstairs bathroom and left it there. I moved it into the attic last week and she never noticed. I'm sure she's forgotten about it."

My pizza was getting cold, but I didn't care. I was too excited about becoming an interior decorator.

"We-ell," said Mary Anne.

"Why don't I come over on Saturday?" I suggested. "I'll bring some stuff with me. If you like it, you can use it. If not, we'll think of other things to do to your room."

"OK!" Mary Anne was beginning to sound more enthusiastic. And I understood how she felt. I love starting new projects.

Later, as I ate my pizza, I made a mental list of things to bring to the Spiers' on Saturday: posters, picture frames, reading lamp, throw pillows. Was there a bedspread somewhere? I'd have to check.

By Saturday morning, I'd gathered so much stuff together that Mom had to drive me over to the Spiers'. This was pretty cagey on my part, since it served three purposes: 1) I got a ride; 2) When Mary Anne saw my mother, she'd know it was OK to use our things; 3) It would give my mom and Mary Anne's dad a chance to see each other.

Unfortunately, Mary Anne's father wasn't home when we got to her house. At least I had a ride, though. And as Mom helped me carry the boxes inside, she said to Mary Anne, "I hope you can use these things. We don't have room for them, and I'd rather see them go to someone we know than to strangers or to the dump."

Mary Anne looked relieved. "Thanks a lot, Mrs Schafer. Really," she said. "This is so nice of you. The cheaper we can redecorate my room, the happier Dad will be."

My mother smiled. "I remember that about your dad," she said fondly. "Kind of tight with a penny."

"Pretty tight with dollars, too," said Mary Anne. "In fact, the more dollars, the tighter he gets."

We laughed. Then Mom left, and Mary Anne and I carried the boxes up to her room. We put them on her bed and settled ourselves next to them.

Mary Anne pulled three rolled-up posters out of one box.

"Let's see what those are," I said. "I don't even remember."

Mary Anne slipped off the rubber bands.

Carefully she unrolled one poster. "Oh!" she cried. "London at night!" (That's what was written under the picture.) "How pretty. Look at all the lights. I had wanted to put up a poster of New York or Paris, but London is just as good. Was this yours? I mean, did it used to be in your room?"

"Nope," I said. "That was in the kitchen, believe it or not. Our kitchen in California was huge."

Mary Anne set aside the poster of London and reached for another poster. She unrolled it and stared at it. She turned it upside down and stared some more.

"Let's see," I said.

Mary Anne turned the poster around. "It's some kind of chart—"

"Hey! That was my dad's astronomy chart. I guess he didn't want it. Those are all the constellations and stars and planets. Do you like it?"

"Yeah," she said slowly. "It's interesting, but I don't know if it's really *me*."

"Well, you don't have to decide about anything just yet."

We continued going through the boxes. After about fifteen minutes, we heard a voice shout, "Hey, you guys! What are you doing?"

We looked out of Mary Anne's open bedroom window – and right into Kristy's open bedroom window next door.

"Hi, Kristy!" called Mary Anne. "We're redecorating my room." She glanced at me. "OK if I ask her over?" she whispered.

"Sure," I replied.

"Want to come over?" she yelled.

"OK."

"Let yourself in," Mary Anne told her. "Dad's not home."

Kristy disappeared from her window. A few minutes later, we heard the Spiers' front door open and close, and then the sound of feet running up the stairs. "Hi," said Kristy. "Gosh, what's all this stuff?"

"Dawn brought it over," Mary Anne replied. "It's from their old house in California. They don't need it any more. Dawn thought I could use it in here. Dad's letting me take the baby stuff – Alice in Wonderland and Humpty Dumpty – off my walls and put up things I want – posters, a photo of the club members, if I could get one."

"He's letting you put drawing pins in the walls?" asked Kristy incredulously.

"I guess so."

Kristy brushed her messy brown hair out of her eyes. "How come you didn't tell *me* you were going to start redecorating?"

"I don't know," Mary Anne answered hesitantly.

Kristy turned to me, but she continued to talk to Mary Anne. "You know, I might have some things you could use, too. Remember last year when we made that poster for art class and it won the prize? You could put that up. I still have it."

"You *do*?" cried Mary Anne. "That would be great! We had fun making that."

"And you know that stencil kit Watson gave me?" she went on.

"Yeah?" said Mary Anne excitedly.

"We could paint those awful pink picture frames and then stencil designs on them."

"Oh, great!"

Kristy smirked at me.

I felt completely left out. After that, the three of us worked on Mary Anne's room for hours. We talked and planned and giggled. But I noticed two things: 1) Kristy only spoke directly to Mary Anne; 2) Kristy never laughed at my jokes. (Even though Mary Anne did.)

I was beginning to worry. I didn't think Kristy liked me very much, and that was not a good situation, since I was a member of the Babysitters Club – and she was the president.

Chapter 4

The first time I met Mary Anne Spier, she was sitting at a table all by herself in the canteen. It was my second day at Stoneybrook Middle School, my fourth day in Connecticut. The members of the Babysitters Club had just had a huge fight and were mad at each other. They weren't even speaking. They were all sitting with other friends – except for Mary Anne, who didn't have any other friends.

Ordinarily, Mary Anne sat with Kristy and the Shillaber twins. Now that she and Kristy are friends again, they're back to their usual lunch group. Sometimes I join them, sometimes I join Claudia and Stacey, who sit with a different crowd – girls *and* boys. Kristy and Mary Anne think boys are dumb. Stacey and Claudia love them. I'm deciding.

The Monday after I helped Mary Anne redecorate her room, I sat with her, Kristy, and

Mariah and Miranda (the twins), even though Kristy was giving me some pretty chilly looks.

The four of us spread our lunches out. The twins had bought the hot lunch. Ew, ew, ew. It was a greyish tuna salad, potato chips, limp green beans, a ice lolly and milk.

Kristy and Mary Anne and I had brought our lunches. Kristy's and Mary Anne's were the same. They had each brought a peanut butter and jam sandwich, an apple, a bag of Doritos and a box of fruit juice. They brought that lunch almost every day. It must be the Connecticut state lunch or something.

It was nothing like what I'd brought.

"What's that you've got?" asked Kristy, pointing to my lunch.

I opened a Tupperware container. "Tofu salad." I unwrapped some foil pouches. "And dried apple rings, a granola bar and some grapefruit."

I saw Kristy and Miranda exchange looks.

Mary Anne saw it, too. She glanced at me and shrugged.

"It's very healthy," I added.

"I know," said Kristy. "Your lunches always are. They're very California, too."

"And yours are quite Connecticut," I said.

I decided to change the subject. If Kristy

wanted me to feel left out for some reason, I could do the same to her. I sighed dreamily.

"What is it?" asked Mariah.

"Oh . . . Mary Anne's dad and my mom went out on another date this weekend. On two, actually."

That got the twins' attention. "They *did*?!" they squealed at the same time.

Mary Anne and I nodded. We looked at each other and smiled.

Kristy scowled.

"Where'd they go?" asked Miranda.

"Out to dinner and the movies on Saturday night, and then out to brunch the very next morning."

"You know something?" said Miranda suddenly. "If your parents got married, you two" (Miranda nodded at Mary Anne and me) "would be *stepsisters*."

A hush fell over our table. Nobody could speak.

Mary Anne and I looked at each other. We were agape. I knew my eyes couldn't be open any wider than hers, because if they were, they'd be stretched up to the moon.

Stepsisters! Why hadn't that occurred to us?

"I never thought of that," I said softly.

"Me neither," said Mary Anne.

"I did," Kristy mumbled.

"It would be almost as good as being twins," said Mariah.

"I'd have a brother *and* a sister!" I exclaimed.

"I've always wanted a sister," said Mary Anne.

"I thought *I* was like your sister," said Kristy.

Everyone ignored her. Everyone but me. I watched Kristy carefully for a few moments. She looked small and hurt. And suddenly I *knew*.

Kristy wasn't mad at me. She didn't dislike me. She was *jealous*. She used to be Mary Anne's best and only friend, but now Mary Anne had me, too. She didn't need Kristy so much any more. Kristy was trying to make me feel left out because she already felt left out.

I remembered how I had taken over when Mary Anne wanted to redo her room. I had jumped in and organized things. We hadn't even asked Kristy over. And, of course, before I came to Connecticut, Kristy would have been the one in charge. No two ways about it.

I felt terrible. What could I do to make Kristy feel better? And if she felt better, would she be nicer to me?

Without knowing it, Mariah gave me a hand.

"Maybe they'll get married and have a big,

beautiful wedding. Everything will be white and beautiful. And there'll be flowers all over the place," she said.

"Your mother's going to get married soon, isn't she, Kristy?" I asked.

Kristy shot me a surprised and grateful look. "In the autumn, probably," she replied.

"And then you'll have a little stepsister and a little stepbrother, right?"

"Right. Plus my three real brothers."

"Gosh, you're going to be a big family," I commented.

"Yeah," added Mary Anne, jumping in. "Four brothers and your first sister."

Kristy nodded happily. "Karen and Andrew are great."

"How's everybody going to fit in your house?" asked Miranda.

It was a good question. The Thomases' house isn't all that big. There *are* four bedrooms, but David Michael's room is more like a cupboard. In fact, it used to be a storage alcove off the hall upstairs.

"Oh," said Kristy, "Karen and Andrew won't live with us. They live with their mother. Watson just gets them every other weekend, every other holiday, and for a couple of weeks each summer."

"But where will they stay when they're visiting?" asked Miranda.

"Actually," Kristy replied, "we don't have to make room for them. We're sort of moving."

"To a mansion," I said.

"A real mansion?" asked Miranda.

"A real mansion," said Kristy.

"I've been there," added Mary Anne. "It really is gigantic. Are you each going to get your own bedroom?"

"Sure," replied Kristy. "There are nine bedrooms in Watson's house."

"Do you get to redecorate? I mean, can you choose the curtains and wallpaper and all?"

Kristy shrugged. "I guess. What I really want is exactly what's in my room right now."

Kristy was beginning to look less than thrilled, so I made one more stab at being friendly. "Kristy and I are helping Mary Anne redecorate her room," I said.

The twins didn't seem to have heard. "How come you want what's in your room right now?" Mariah asked Kristy. "You've had that for years."

I poked at my tofu salad. "Just think," I said. "You could probably do anything you wanted to your new room. High tech or. . ."

Kristy was eating her sandwich. (She looked

more like she wanted to kill it.) Very slowly, she put the crusts down on her paper napkin.

She brushed the crumbs off her hands.

Then she turned to look at me. "What I want," she said coolly, "is what I've got – where it is. So lay off, OK?"

"OK," I said, frowning.

"Good." With that, Kristy stood up, stuffed her trash in her brown bag, scrunched up the bag, and left. "See you guys later," she said over her shoulder.

"Later," said Mariah and Miranda.

I looked at Mary Anne. I wanted to say, "What'd I do?" but before I could ask the question, Mary Anne said simply, "She doesn't want to move."

"Oh," I replied. I had made another mistake. And then, "*Oh.*" Kristy was letting me know that I was still an outsider, at least at *her* lunch table.

After school that day, I went over to Mary Anne's house. The sunshine was warm on my shoulders as we walked along.

"Almost like California," I told her. "Like California in December. But that's OK. It's better than nothing."

"You really miss it, don't you?" Mary Anne said. "California, I mean."

"Yeah, I really do. I suppose if I'd grown up here in Stoneybrook, I'd be happy here and love the weather. But I didn't and I'm not, so I don't."

"You're not happy?" Mary Anne asked. She looked disappointed.

"Oh," I said, "I'm not *un*happy. I just miss things, that's all. Think how you'd feel if your father suddenly moved you to California. You'd probably hate it. At least at first."

"I guess you're right. But I want you to be happy here."

"Hey!" I said. I smiled. "I'm not complaining – about anything except the weather. You're great, your friends are great, the Babysitters Club is great. And between us, you and I might end up with a whole family again. What more could I ask for?"

"A million bucks?" Mary Anne suggested.

"That'd be nice. And maybe a swimming pool."

"And no more school."

"And thirty-degree weather all year round."

"And a lifetime supply of ice cream."

"And a pet baboon."

Mary Anne giggled. "And . . . and. . . Hey, there's Kristy! Just up ahead. Kristy! Kristy!" she called.

Kristy turned around. "Yeah?"

"Wait up!" Mary Anne shouted. We ran to catch up to Kristy.

Even as we were running, I could see that Kristy was not pleased to see us. At any rate, she wasn't pleased to see me. I'm sure she thought I was hogging Mary Anne again.

"Hi," said Mary Anne, as we reached Kristy. "Are you babysitting this afternoon?"

"Yeah, for Jamie. What are you guys doing?"

"We're. . . " Mary Anne started to say. "We're. . ." She didn't know how to finish the sentence.

The problem was that we were going to work on her room some more, and she had realized that that was a touchy subject.

"Going to work on your room?" asked Kristy.

Mary Anne nodded.

"I thought so."

I shifted from one foot to the other. "Too bad you're babysitting," I said. "If you weren't, you could help us."

"Yeah, too bad," Kristy said sarcastically.

I glanced at Mary Anne.

She looked at me and shrugged.

"Want to help us tomorrow?" I asked.

"Can't. I'm sitting for David Michael."

Mary Anne looked at the ground.

"Well," I said, after a pause, "we'll see you at the meeting this afternoon. Have fun."

"OK. See you." Kristy turned into the Newtons' driveway, leaving us behind.

I looked at Mary Anne. She looked at me.

"Is she mad?" Mary Anne asked, nodding toward Kristy.

"Nope," I replied. "She's jealous."

Chapter 5

On the afternoon of Tuesday, April 28, I let out a cheer and congratulated the weatherman from WSTO (the local radio station). He was the one who said the day before that the weather would turn sunny and the temperature would rise to twenty-six.

He was right.

Maybe there would be summer in Connecticut after all.

I took the beautiful weather as a sign that things would go well when I babysat for the club's new clients that afternoon. It was my day to take care of Buddy, Suzi and Marnie Barrett, and I was looking forward to it.

When I rang the Barretts' bell that afternoon, the door was opened by Suzi, looking timid.

"Hi, Suzi," I said. "I'm Dawn. I fixed your knee. Do you remember?"

She nodded.

"Well, I'm going to babysit for you today. Is your mom here?"

Suzi nodded again.

At that moment a small, curly blonde head peeped around Suzi.

"Marnie?" I guessed.

Suzi nodded.

"May I come in?" I asked finally.

Suzi nodded.

I stepped into the hallway. "Hello?" I called.

"YAH! YAH! Bang-bang-bang!"

I jumped a mile as Buddy, wearing a cowboy hat and swimming flippers, galloped out of the living room. He was pointing a ray gun at me.

"Shpoof! You're burned! You're a goner!" he cried.

I raised an eyebrow. Then, ever so casually, I leaned over and took the gun from him. "Hello," I said. "I'm Dawn Schafer. I met you at the Pikes'. And I'm your babysitter. I don't like guns. So no guns when I'm around. That goes for you guys, too," I told Suzi and Marnie.

Suzi nodded.

Marnie stared at me with wide blue eyes.

I noticed that Suzi's jumper was coming unbuttoned, and that Marnie's nappies were drooping and the hem was falling out of her overalls. A grubby bandage was wrapped around one of Buddy's fingers. All three kids needed to have their hair brushed.

I looked in the living room. It was a sight. Newspapers and toys were scattered everywhere. A plateful of crumbs sat under a lamp. Something red had been spilled on the coffee table and hadn't been wiped up. Our house might have been disorganized, but the Barretts' house was a pigsty.

I dared to glance in the kitchen. What a mistake. The sink was overflowing with pots and dishes, napkins and ice lolly wrappers, and about a million TV dinner trays. The breakfast dishes were still on the table. I could tell exactly what Mrs Barrett had served because the remains were in plain view. Soft-boiled eggs (the yolks, now crusty, glued to the plates), orange juice (dried pulp in the glasses), bananas (peels on the table) and Pop-Tarts (crusts stuck in a glass).

Yick. Ew, ew, ew.

I was still looking around when I heard footsteps on the stairs. I turned and saw an absolutely gorgeous young woman rushing towards us. She looked like a model. Honest. She was wearing a silk blouse, a sleek linen suit, brown heels and gold jewellery – not too much, but enough so you noticed it. Her hair fell away from her face in chestnut curls and she smelled of a heavenly perfume.

"Dawn?" she asked breathlessly.

"Yes. Hi, Mrs Barrett."

"Thank you for coming." She flashed me a warm smile, then quickly kissed Marnie, Suzi and Buddy in turn.

"So long, darlings. Be good for Dawn." She rushed to the front door.

"Wait!" I called. "Where are you going to be?"

"On a job interview. And I'm late. Buddy, be a sweetheart and let Pow in the back door. I can hear him whining." Mrs Barrett was halfway down the walk.

"Hey, what am I supposed to do this afternoon?" Where were the special instructions? Snack time at four o'clock or help with homework, or *some*thing.

Mrs Barrett paused. For a moment her beautiful face looked confused. "Just . . . sit," she said.

"What if – what if there's an emergency?" I asked. "How do I reach you?"

"I'll be at Mason and Company. It's on Spring Street. Or call the Pikes, OK?"

"Well . . ." (Mrs Barrett's car zoomed backwards down the drive.) ". . . all right," I finished, as she waved to us from the window and sped away.

I looked at the Barrett kids. They looked at me.

"You guys ever see *Mary Poppins*?" I asked.

They shook their heads.

Darn. I'd thought I could get them to tidy up the living room by pretending we were Mary Poppins and Jane and Michael Banks, cleaning up the nursery.

"Well, how'd you like to surprise your mother?"

"OK!" said Buddy. I could tell he'd do anything for her.

"We're going to surprise her with a clean house."

"We are?" asked Buddy suspiciously.

"Yup. First go let Pow in, then I'll tell you what we're going to do."

"All right."

Buddy disappeared. While he was gone, I buttoned Suzi's jumper and rolled up the cuffs of Marnie's overalls. Then I pulled a brush out of my purse and ran it through Marnie's curls. "We'll do your hair later," I told Suzi. "We'll have to take the plaits out first."

Suzi nodded.

Buddy returned, followed by a sleepy-looking basset hound. "This is Pow," he announced. "The meanest dog that ever lived."

Pow's eyelids drooped. He rolled over on his side. "Are you sure?" I asked.

"Yup," replied Buddy.

"This must be an off day," I said as Pow fell asleep. "OK, you guys, are you ready for a game? I'm going to time us to see how fast we can clean up the living room. Take anything that doesn't belong in there and put it where it does belong. Tidy everything else up. But be careful. Don't work so fast you break something. We'll have to add time to our score if we break anything." I looked at my watch. The second hand was approaching the twelve.

"Take your marks." Suzi and Buddy and I crowded into the doorway of the living room. Buddy removed the swimming flippers. (Marnie didn't know what was going on.)

"Get set."

We crouched down.

"GO!"

We ran into the living room and a flurry of activity began. Buddy found three plates and ran them into the kitchen.

"Bring the sponge back with you!" I yelled.

Buddy returned and threw me the sponge. I wiped up the coffee table while Suzi collected newspapers.

"Does your mom save the papers?" I asked.

Suzi shook her head.

"Then stack them up," I told her. "We'll make a bundle for the recycling collector." Suzi stacked, I straightened cushions, Buddy rounded up toys and Marnie helped him.

Within minutes the room looked as if it belonged in a different house, or maybe even in a TV commercial. I checked my watch. "Six minutes and seventeen seconds!" I announced.

"Is that a record?" exclaimed Buddy.

"It might be," I said. "But not if we break it cleaning up the kitchen. Shall we try to break our record?"

"Yes, yes, yes!" shouted Buddy.

Suzi smiled shyly at me. Her eyes were shining.

Marnie scrunched up her face and wrinkled her nose.

"That's the ham face," Buddy informed me. "She only makes it when she's happy."

I grinned. "All right, everybody, here are the special instructions for the Kitchen Race. I'm in charge of putting dishes in the dishwasher. You guys bring dirty dishes to me and I'll take care of them. Rubbish goes in the bin, and anything that doesn't belong in the kitchen goes to the room it does belong in. Got it?"

"Got it," said Buddy.

"Got it," said Suzi.

Marnie made the ham face.

"Take your marks," I cried. "Get set, go!"

The kitchen was tougher than the living room. It took longer than I had thought it would to rinse the plates and glasses and put them in the dishwasher, but we worked hard anyway. Suzi cleaned the rubbish out of the sink and put it in the bin. Buddy swept the floor. Marnie found a bag of M&Ms and began eating them. I stopped her, gave her a paper towel and showed her how to mop up the floor around Pow's water bowl.

When we were done, I looked at my watch again. "Well, we didn't break our record, I'm afraid. That took eleven minutes and forty-eight seconds."

"Darn," said Buddy.

"Yeah, darn," said Suzi.

"Let's clean up the playroom," Buddy suggested. "That's a real mess. If we break the record in there, it'll be a miracle."

So we straightened up the playroom, too. (We

did not break our record.) Mrs Barrett wasn't going to recognize her own house when she got home.

The Barrett kids and I flopped on the couch in the playroom. Pow wandered in. Buddy aimed a finger at him. "Blam, blam!" he shrieked.

I covered Buddy's hand with my own. "Hey, remember what I said about guns," I warned him. "Not while I'm around."

"So? Who says you're the boss?" Buddy asked defiantly. He leaped up and stood in front of me, legs spread, cowboy hat askew. Very slowly, he raised his gun finger and aimed it at me.

"Buddy," I said calmly, "while I am babysitting, I am the boss. I'm in charge. And I say no guns."

"Why?"

"Because real guns are very dangerous. They are not toys. And I don't think we should ever pretend they are toys. There are plenty of other things we can pretend instead."

"Like what?"

"Like I'm a hairdresser, and you're a father, and Suzi and Marnie are your kids and you decide to take them to get their hair cut."

Buddy considered this. "I'm the daddy?" he asked.

"Yup."

"I'm the boss of them?" He pointed to his sisters.

"Yup."

"OK."

So I accomplished two things. I replaited Suzi's hair (and even brushed Buddy's), and I took Buddy's mind off guns. Buddy wasn't going to be playing with guns while I was around.

By five o'clock, the kids were getting tired and cranky. Buddy yelled at Pow. Marnie stopped making the ham face. Suzi stopped talking and started nodding again.

"Do you have a daddy?" Buddy asked me suddenly.

We were sitting on the floor in the playroom. I looked at him in surprise. "Well, yes," I replied. "But not here. I mean, he doesn't live with us."

"Really?" said Buddy.

I sighed. "Yeah. He's in California. Three thousand miles away."

Buddy nodded knowingly. He looked like a little old man. "We don't have our daddy, either."

"My mom and dad are divorced," I explained.

"So are ours," said Buddy.

"I know."

Suzi had been helping Marnie build a tower of paper cups. She looked up with interest. "I wonder how long divorce lasts," she said.

"It's for ever," I replied, surprised.

"That's what Mommy said, but. . ."

"But you keep hoping your dad will come back?"

"Yeah," said Buddy and Suzi at the same time.

"Me, too," I said, "except I know he won't."

"Do you miss your dad?" asked Buddy.

"Very much."

"Me, too."

Buddy moved over until he was sitting next to me. I put my arm around him. Then I held my other arm out to Suzi, but instead of joining us, she jumped to her feet.

"You. Are. A. Liar!" she cried, pointing her finger at me. "A *liar*." Then she ran out of the playroom and upstairs.

"What did I say?" I asked Buddy.

Buddy frowned. "I think it was the part about daddies not coming back. She *really* thinks ours is going to come home for good one day."

"Hmm," I said. "Well, we'll leave her alone for a while."

Buddy turned on a cartoon show and settled down to watch. After a while I decided to take Marnie upstairs to change her nappy. Marnie shared a room with Suzi, but Suzi wasn't in the room. The door to the bathroom was closed, however.

As I was finishing up with Marnie, the bathroom door opened a crack. Suzi peeked through. "Dawn?" she asked.

"Yeah?"

"I-I had an accident." Suzi scrunched up her face and began to cry.

"Hey, that's OK," I said. "Accidents happen." I put Marnie in her crib, and stepped into the bathroom, closing the door behind me.

"I wet my pants," Suzi moaned.

"It's really all right," I told her. I grabbed some paper towels and mopped up the puddle on the tile floor.

"Do we have to tell Mommy?" asked Suzi.

"Not if you don't want to. Here, we'll rinse out your trousers and your underwear, and get you some clean trousers. Then you'll be all set."

By the time Suzi and Marnie and I were on our way downstairs, Suzi was smiling again. A few minutes later, Mrs Barrett came home. I wish I'd had a camera so I could have recorded the look on her face when she saw the clean house.

"You're a wonder, Dawn!" she exclaimed.

"She's the best babysitter we ever had," said Buddy.

"She's our favourite," Suzi chimed in.

"I hope you'll come back," said Mrs Barrett as she paid me.

"Any time," I told her cheerfully.

If I had only known then how often "any time" was going to be, I might not have spoken so quickly.

Chapter 6

Saturday, May 2

I babysat for Karen and Andrew for four hours this afternoon. Karen invited a friend over and the four of us played "Let's All Come In". We had a scary encounter with Mrs Porter and she did some witchy things, but nothing happened. Boo-Boo is terrified of her now and stays inside, so there weren't any problems. He slept in one of the first-floor bedrooms most of the afternoon. Karen says he used to go on the second floor, but that their attic is haunted, so he won't go any higher than the first storey. Karen's got a real thing about this haunted attic, which *you guys should be aware of when you sit at Watson's. I'm trying to convince her it's not haunted – without actually having to go in it myself.*

Kristy is so lucky. I wish Andrew and Karen were going to be *my* little stepsister and stepbrother. I babysat for them once and they were lots of fun and really cute, even if Andrew is kind of shy and Karen talks too much.

I asked Kristy lots of questions about her afternoon there because I was trying extra hard to be friendly to her. Kristy always opens up where Andrew and Karen are concerned. This is what she told me.

As soon as Mr Brewer left, Karen pulled Kristy into the living room and said, "Let's play 'Let's All Come In'. *Please.*"

"OK," said Kristy, "but I don't think we really have enough people. Wouldn't the game be better with four?"

"Let's All Come In" is a game Karen invented herself. Karen just turned six and she's very smart. She started out in kindergarten last autumn and was skipped into first grade after Christmas. She didn't have a bit of trouble, and now she reads like crazy and can add and subtract almost as fast as I can.

Her game is about the guests who come to a big, fancy, old-fashioned hotel. Karen always makes Kristy (or the oldest person) the senior porter. Then she and Andrew and her friends take turns entering the lobby as hotel workers or exotic guests – wealthy old women in furs, sea captains, famous people. Karen and Andrew have an amazing collection of "dress-up" clothes, so they can put on a good costume for just about every character. And Mr Brewer's living room is perfect for a lobby.

As I've mentioned, Mr Brewer is rich and his house is a mansion. It's full of expensive things, but he hasn't turned it into a museum. What I mean is that Karen and Andrew are allowed in the living room, the dining room, the study, etc., even though there are antiques and breakables everywhere. As far as I know, they're always careful. Maybe it's because they know their father trusts them.

Anyway, Mr Brewer's living room is gigantic – big enough for a grand piano, and even a little tree, which stands in a brass tub near the fireplace. There are three couches, five armchairs, a long glass coffee table, several end tables and a crystal chandelier. Instead of carpeting, Mr Brewer has put small Oriental rugs down and keeps the wooden floor polished. The room does look a little like a hotel lobby, if you squint your eyes and use your imagination, which Kristy and Karen and even Andrew (although he's not quite four) can do just fine.

"I know who the fourth person for our game could be," Karen told Kristy that Saturday afternoon.

"Who?"

"Hannie Papadakis."

Hannie is one of Karen's new first-grade friends. She lives across the street and two mansions down from the Brewers. Kristy had met Hannie a couple of times and liked her.

"OK," said Kristy. "Let's call her. You invite her over, but I'll have to talk to her mother or father."

(A good babysitter always includes parents in plans for younger children. Kristy knew that Mr and Mrs Papadakis might not want Hannie going to a house with a babysitter in charge instead of a parent.)

But Mr Papadakis said it was fine for Hannie to come over, and a few minutes later, Hannie was ringing the Brewers' front bell.

Karen and Andrew ran to answer it.

"See who's there before you open the door," Kristy cautioned them. (You can't be too careful.)

Karen peered out of the left window, Andrew peered out of the right. "It's Hannie!" they called at the same time.

"OK, let her in."

Karen hauled open the door and led Hannie into the living room. "Are you ready for 'Let's All Come In'?" Karen asked her excitedly. "That's what we're playing today." Sometimes Karen can be bossy. I'm surprised she and Kristy get along so well.

"I'm all ready," replied Hannie, who has played often. "First I'm going to be Mrs Noswimple."

"OK," said Karen. "Kristy, you go behind the desk. Andrew, you be the porter."

As the youngest, Andrew often gets stuck with parts like lift operator or porter, or less important characters such as somebody's little boy. Once, Karen made him play a pet cocker spaniel.

Kristy sat on the floor behind the coffee table. Karen had placed a pencil, a composition book and a bell in front of her.

"Hannie, come put on your Mrs Noswimple outfit. Andrew, get your cap and jacket."

The kids ran up the stairs to the playroom

on the first floor. A few minutes later, they ran back down. Andrew was wearing a red cap and a blue jacket decorated with gold braid. Hannie was wearing a skirt that reached to the floor; large, sparkly high heels with no toes; a fur stole; and a hat with a veil. In one hand, she carried a pair of spectacles attached to a diamond-studded stick. Behind her, Karen was dressed as Mrs Mysterious, all in black, including a black eye patch and a black fright wig.

"Places, you guys!" Karen directed.

Andrew ran to stand next to Kristy's "desk", Karen waited in the foyer since guests only come into the hotel one at a time, and Hannie made her entrance.

She walked into the hotel lobby as grandly as was possible, considering she was clumping around in shoes that were six sizes too big for her. "Hell*oo*," she called in a high, thin voice.

"Good day," replied Kristy. "Won't you come in, Mrs Noswimple. How nice to see you."

"Why, thank you," replied Hannie. "I'm just staying for one night this time, Mr Steve Potter." (Hannie has never once pronounced "senior porter" properly.) "I'm meeting my husband in Canada tomorrow. We're going to go to a party with the queen. And the emperor."

"How lovely," said Kristy. "Does the emperor have new clothes?"

"Oh, yes. He has a new suit of silver," replied Hannie, not getting the joke.

"Oh," said Kristy. "Well, why don't you sign the registration book and then the porter here will help you to your room."

"OK." Hannie bent over the composition book, pencil poised. "Kristy," she whispered, "how do you spell 'Noswimple'?"

Kristy spelled it out and Hannie printed the name painstakingly. She straightened up. "Ready, porter? I have two trunks and a hatbox, so I need lots of help."

"Ready, Mrs Noswimple," said Andrew.

Andrew and Hannie left the living room and Karen entered.

"I don't believe it!" cried Kristy. "Mrs Mysterious! What a surprise! How nice to see you. You haven't stopped by in ages."

"Heh, heh," cackled Karen. "I've been at a Mysterious Meeting in Transylvania. All the witches and warlocks and ghosts and spooks and mysterious people got together."

"Well, you're looking especially mysterious today," said Kristy.

"Thank you," Karen answered politely. "I do

look mysterious, don't I." It was a statement, not a question. Karen stepped over to one of the floor-to-ceiling windows that look out on the Brewers' front lawn. "This is a mirror," she told Kristy. "I'll just—"

Karen stopped midsentence. She shrieked.

So did Kristy.

Andrew and Hannie ran into the living room to see what was happening. Andrew gasped and hid behind an armchair. Hannie opened her eyes and mouth wide, but couldn't make a sound.

Kristy told me later that she was so surprised she thought she was going to faint.

What everyone had seen when Karen stepped in front of her "mirror" was another scary, black-clad figure. Only it wasn't Karen's reflection. It was someone outside the window – Mrs Porter from next door.

The thing about Mrs Porter is that Karen is convinced she's a witch whose real name is Morbidda Destiny. Karen's got everyone – Andrew, Hannie, Kristy and all us Babysitters (especially Mary Anne) thinking she's a witch, too. So it was no wonder everyone panicked.

Mrs Porter gestured towards the front door with a wave of her cape. "Yipes," said Kristy, heart pounding. "I wonder what she wants."

"Probably frogs' noses or the hair from a mole or something. I bet she's cooking," Karen offered.

"Don't be silly," said Kristy.

With legs that felt as heavy as lead, Kristy opened the front door – just a crack.

Mrs Porter was standing on the front steps. She was leaning over so that her nose poked into Kristy's face.

Kristy jumped back.

"I rang your bell," Mrs Porter said in a croaky voice, "but you didn't answer."

"Sometimes it doesn't work," Karen spoke up timidly from where she was hiding behind Kristy.

"Can – can I help you?" Kristy asked. The last time Mrs Porter had come to the door, it was to dump poor fat old Boo-Boo, the Brewers' cat, inside after he had left the remains of a mouse on Mrs Porter's front porch.

"I'm cooking. I need to borrow something."

Kristy noticed that Mrs Porter had a little scar near the corner of her mouth that jumped around when she spoke.

Karen nudged Kristy's back. "I told you so," she whispered. "Morbidda Destiny is *cooking*."

Kristy nudged Karen back. "What do you need, Mrs Porter?"

"Fennel and coriander."

"Aughh!" screamed Karen.

"Aughh!" screamed Andrew and Hannie, who were watching from the safety of the living room.

"Shh," said Kristy. "They're just herbs, you guys." She turned back to Mrs Porter. "I'm really sorry, but I'm sure Mr Brewer doesn't have those things. He's not much of a cook."

"Well, it never hurts to ask." Mrs Porter turned abruptly and dashed down the front steps and across the lawn towards her house. Her black cape and dress flapped in the breeze.

Karen, Andrew and Hannie found the courage to run to the front door and watch her leave. Kristy watched with them. They saw her pause at her herb garden and examine the new green shoots. They saw her flap up the steps to her own front porch. And they all saw her take up a broom and carry it into the house, talking to it.

Kristy closed the door before the kids could panic again. As she did so, something occurred to her. "Karen," she said, "where's Boo-Boo?"

"Well," replied Karen, "I'm not sure. But he's probably upstairs. I'll show you where." Karen ran upstairs, the others at her heels.

She ran down the long hallway past the playroom, past her room, past Andrew's room, and past two guest rooms to a room at the end of the hall.

Kristy looked inside. Curled up at the foot of the bed was Boo-Boo, the world's fattest cat.

"Oh, good," said Kristy with a sigh. "I was afraid he might be out in Mrs Porter's garden again."

"Nope," said Karen. "He's scared of her now. He stays inside all day. Mostly he stays right here. And he never goes up to the second floor any more. You know why?"

"Why? I'm afraid to ask."

"Because the attic is haunted."

"Karen. . ." Kristy warned.

"It is?" said Hannie in amazement.

Karen nodded solemnly. "Animals know those things. Our attic is haunted. It's haunted by the ghost of old Ben Brewer, Daddy's great-grandfather, who—"

Kristy cut Karen off. Karen's imagination frequently ran away, and when it did, it took Andrew and Hannie along with it. "Come on, you guys. Let's go back to 'Let's All Come In'."

So the kids returned to the living room and took up the game again. They were still playing when Mr Brewer came home.

Kristy sighed as she left. She'd had fun. But she was pretty sure she hadn't heard the last about old Ben Brewer.

Chapter 7

I had to do something about Kristy. I was trying my hardest to be nice to her, but things were no better between us. So one day at school, out of the clear blue, I said to her, "Want to come over to my house this afternoon?" I didn't even know I was going to say it. It just slipped out. I was as surprised as Kristy was.

And we were both pretty surprised when she replied, "OK. Sure."

What had I got myself into? What would Kristy and I do? Every time we talked, it turned into an argument. Well, I thought, we could always watch a movie. I hadn't seen *The Sound of Music* in a while.

After school that day, I met Kristy and we walked to my house together. Mary Anne didn't walk with us. She was babysitting for Charlotte Johanssen, and the Johanssens live in the opposite direction from me. That was just as well, since

Mary Anne is sort of the cause of our problems. Kristy and I needed some time alone together.

At first we walked along in silence. Kristy stared at the ground. She didn't look mad, but I felt uncomfortable being silent with her.

"We live in an old farmhouse," I told her, just to make conversation. "It was built in seventeen ninety-five."

"Oh, yeah?" said Kristy.

Was she interested, or did she think I was bragging?

"Yeah," I replied uncertainly.

"Do you like it?"

"Mostly. It's neat living in a place that old. But the rooms are kind of small and the doorways are low. The first time Mary Anne came over, she said the colonists must have been midgets."

Kristy burst out laughing. Then she caught herself and scowled. She pressed her lips into two straight lines. Thin lips are never a good sign.

I cringed. How could I have mentioned Mary Anne? I really hadn't meant to.

I went on about the house some more. "When the house was first built," I said, "there was nothing but farmland for miles around it. But Stoneybrook kept growing, and the people who owned the house kept selling off land until finally there were just one and a half acres left, with the house, an outhouse, a barn, and an old smokehouse. It sort of got run-down. By the time my mom bought the place, nobody had lived on the property for two years. We got it cheap."

"You have a barn on your property?" Kristy asked with interest.

"Mm-hmm."

"Do you play in it?"

"Well," I said, "we're not supposed to go in it too much, but sometimes my brother and I play there."

"Why aren't you supposed to go in it?"

"Because it's so old. Mom's afraid the roof will come crashing down sometime. She may be right."

"You don't have any animals, do you?" asked Kristy.

"You mean in the barn?" I shook my head. "But the people who lived there before us must have. There are still bales of hay sitting around, and there's tons of hay in the hayloft. Sometimes Jeff – that's my brother – and I go up in the loft. There are great places to hide, and we rigged up a rope so that we can swing down from this beam way high up under the roof, and land in the hay."

"*Really?*" said Kristy.

"Yup."

She paused. Then she said, "I guess you and Mary Anne play in the barn all the time."

"Mary Anne?" I exclaimed. "Not a chance. She won't jump off the beam into the hayloft. She won't even go inside because of what Mom said about the roof. She may have changed this spring, but not that much."

Kristy looked at me and grinned.

When we got home, the front door was locked, so I let myself in with the key. Back in California, I never needed a key. Mom was always home. Now I'm in danger of becoming a latchkey kid.

I almost said so, but luckily remembered just in time that Kristy has been a latchkey kid for years. Instead I said, "I wonder where my mom went."

We found out as soon as we walked into the kitchen. Stuck to the refrigerator with a magnet shaped like a pair of lips was a note that said:

Hi, kids! I've gone on two job interviews. Back at five. Love, Mom. P.S. Do not, under any circumstances, touch the tofu-ginger salad in the refrigerator.

Kristy looked at me, wide-eyed. "You mean there's a chance someone would?"

I tried to glare at her, but it turned into a smile. "Yes," I replied. "We all happen to love tofu-ginger salad. It's good. . . *Really*," I added, as Kristy made gagging noises.

I looked helplessly around the kitchen. "You're probably hungry, aren't you?"

"Starved," Kristy said. "But-but not so starved I'd eat tofu or sunflower seeds or something. I don't suppose you have any peanut butter."

"Sugar-free and unsalted, made from organically grown peanuts."

"That'll do. Any jam or honey?"

"Raw honey. We've already scooped the comb out."

"White bread?"

"High-fibre wheat-and bran."

Kristy made do with the peanut butter, honey and bread. I ate some yoghurt with wheat germ in it.

Jeff came home, ate a banana, and went over to the Pikes' to play with the triplets.

When he was gone, I looked at Kristy. "Well," I said, "what do you want to do? We could watch a movie. Or I could show you my room. Or we could search the house for a secret passageway."

"Could we go in the barn?" asked Kristy.

"Sure," I said. "As long as we're careful."

We ran out of the back door and across the garden to the barn. We didn't even need our jackets since the hayloft gets pretty warm on a sunny day.

The main entrance to the barn (which, I should say, is not a very big barn) is a pair of sliding doors on one end. We leave one of the doors partway open all the time. We've stored some stuff in one of the horse stalls, but nothing that's worth stealing.

Kristy and I stepped through the opening. "Ooh," said Kristy. "It smells . . . like a barn. I mean, even without the animals."

"I know," I said. "Isn't it great? You could almost imagine you were on a big old farm out in the middle of nowhere."

(I think the barn smell comes mostly from the hay.)

We walked down the aisle between two rows of stalls. The stalls had long ago been cleaned out, and the harnesses and tools that had once hung on the walls had been removed, but here and there a nameplate remained.

Kristy read a few of them aloud. "Dobbs, Grey Boy, Cornflower."

Aside from the stalls and some old feeding troughs, there wasn't much to see.

"How do you get to the hayloft?" asked Kristy.

"This way," I said. I led her to the end of the barn. A ladder was leaning against the loft, which was just a couple of feet above my head.

We climbed up and Kristy walked around in the hay. "Mmm," she said. "It's soft – sort of. And it smells good." She looked up. The roof was high above us. The sun shone through the cracks and caught the dust motes in its light.

"Neat," said Kristy. "It's so *quiet* in here."

"You want to swing from the rope?" I asked.

"Sure. I mean, I think so. How high up is it?"

"I'll show you." A series of wooden blocks were built into the wall above the loft. They went up and up and up. I climbed them until I reached a beam that was twelve feet above the hayloft. (Jeff and I measured once.)

"Swing that rope up to me," I called to Kristy.

Kristy looked doubtfully at the rope, then at me. "All the way up there?" she said.

"Sure, it's easy. Just try it."

Kristy took hold of the end of the rope and swung it over and up.

I missed it by inches.

We tried again and I caught it. "Watch this!" I yelled. Holding on to the knot that Jeff had tied near the bottom of the rope, I pushed away from the wall and sailed out and down. When I had almost reached the other wall of the barn I let go and landed with a thump in the hay. *"Oof.* Oh, that was great! Do you want to try?" I stood up, brushing the hay off my jeans.

"I guess so." Kristy began her ascent. She was climbing the wall awfully slowly.

"You don't have to go all the way to the beam, if you don't want," I told her.

"No – I can do it."

Kristy sat shakily on the beam. I tossed the rope to her. The expression on her face as she flew through the air changed from sheer horror ("Let go! Let go!" I screeched as she approached the opposite wall) to amazement to joy (when she landed).

She sat in the hay for a moment, then leaped up and exclaimed, "Oh, wow! That was terrific!"

We each took five more turns, Kristy looking cockier every time. Then we lay on our backs in the loft, gazing at the roof and watching the sunlight grow dimmer.

We began to talk. We talked about divorces. ("They should be against the law," said Kristy. I agreed.) We talked about moving. ("Across town is nothing compared to across country," I pointed out. Kristy agreed.) We talked about the Babysitters Club. ("It's more important to me than school," I said. Kristy understood.)

Then we talked about Mary Anne. After saying some boring things like how good she looked in her new clothes, Kristy said, "I'm glad she made a new friend."

"Really?" I asked.

"Yes. She needs new friends."

"Well, I'm glad she still has her old friends."

"You know, I've been thinking," said Kristy. "We should have an alternate officer for our club. Somebody who could take over any job if one of us can't be at a meeting. Someone who understands each office. Would you like to be Official Alternate Officer?"

"Definitely!" I replied. And that was how, all in one day, I patched up my problems with Kristy and became Official Alternate Officer of the Babysitters Club.

Chapter 8

The spring was growing warmer and warmer. For several days in a row, the temperature reached thirty degrees. Mary Anne said that this was abnormal, which I took as both good news and bad news.

The good news was that maybe we'd continue to have abnormally warm weather, which would be a kind way to ease me through my first Connecticut springtime. The bad news was that maybe next year we would have an abnormally cool spring (to make up for this year), which would be cruel to my system.

I think I'm cold-blooded.

One of those thirty-degree days was a Saturday, and I had a babysitting job with the Barretts. I had been there several times by then. I was looking forward to the day not only because it was going to be warm (hot!) and because I liked the Barrett kids, but because Stacey and Claudia were going to be sitting down the street at the Pikes', and we had plans to get together with our charges.

The reason both Stacey and Claudia were going to be sitting for the Pikes was because all eight children were going to be there.

Mrs Barrett had asked me to show up at eight fifteen on Saturday morning. Yuck. I like to sleep late. But Mrs Barrett had found a seminar she wanted to go to that would help her with her job search. It was an all-day affair that started at eight-thirty in the morning.

Despite the fact that I had sat at the Barretts' on Thursday – just two days earlier – the house was in its usual messy state when I got there on Saturday. Furthermore, although Mrs Barrett came downstairs looking stunning, Buddy, Suzi and Marnie were still in their pyjamas. Their beds were unmade, they had not eaten breakfast, their hair was a fright and Marnie's nappy badly needed to be changed.

Mrs Barrett didn't mention any of this, though. She didn't give me any instructions, either, just dashed out of the house, saying that the number where she could be reached was taped to the phone. At least she had remembered to do that.

The kids gathered around me in the kitchen and looked at me expectantly. "How long are you staying?" asked Buddy.

"All day," I replied, feeling less than enthusiastic.

"Yay!" cried Buddy and Suzi. They jumped up and down.

Marnie made the ham face.

I felt better.

I changed Marnie's nappy. Then I asked the kids if they were hungry.

"Yes!" chorused Suzi and Buddy.

Well, first things first. I decided to give the kids breakfast. After breakfast I would get them dressed and help them make their beds and clean up their rooms. The day began to take shape. They could play outdoors until about twelve-thirty, then have lunch. Around one-thirty the girls would go down for naps, and maybe I would have a quiet time with Buddy. After that, more playtime, then some races to clean up the living room and playroom.

I made a mental schedule as I settled the kids at the kitchen table. The only thing I forgot to figure in was playing with Claudia, Stacey and the Pike kids.

My mental schedule called for breakfast to be over at 9:15.

At 9:20, Buddy asked for more cereal.

At 9:22, Pow whined to be let in.

At 9:25, Marnie spilled Suzi's orange juice.

At 9:28, Suzi was still yelling at Marnie.

At 9:31, Pow whined to be let out.

At 9:34, I was still cleaning up the table. (The schedule called for the kids to be dressed by 9:45. I revised the schedule, deciding that the kids could be dressed by 10:15, and chopped half an hour off their morning playtime.)

At 9:50, Claudia called and suggested having a picnic lunch in the Pikes' back garden with all the kids. She asked if we could bring sandwiches for ourselves and bake brownies for everyone. She said she thought the picnic should start at one o'clock.

One o'clock! I'd never get Marnie and Suzi down for naps by one-thirty. I revised the afternoon schedule and re-revised the morning schedule, shortening playtime again, then adding brownie-making time. If the kids were dressed and their rooms straightened by ten-thirty, we might be ready for the picnic by one o'clock.

"How would you guys like to have a picnic lunch at the Pikes'?" I asked.

I got a yeah from Buddy, a yeah from Suzi, and a ham face from Marnie.

"OK," I told them. "Then we have a lot to do this morning. You've got to get dressed and pick up your rooms, and – guess what – we're going to make brownies for the picnic!"

"Oh, boy!" cried Buddy. "Can we start right now?"

"Nope," I told him. "Not until you and your sisters are ready for the day."

"We're ready for the day," he said.

"Not in your pyjamas you aren't. Come on, everybody."

Dressing, bed-making, and room-straightening went much more slowly than I could have imagined. I thought about having cleaning races, but decided not to overuse the activity. If I did, it would lose its appeal.

An hour and a half after we'd gone upstairs, the Barretts were "ready for the day". It was eleven-thirty. The picnic started at one o'clock. We had an hour and a half to make brownies. I hoped Mrs B. had brownie mix somewhere, because the kids and I were going to do a lot better working with a mix than working from scratch.

I assembled Buddy, Suzi and Marnie in the kitchen. (I put Marnie in her high chair and gave her a wooden spoon to play with.)

"Aprons for everybody," I announced, pulling three out of a cupboard.

"Not me," exclaimed Buddy. "Aprons are for girls."

"Aprons are for *cooks*," I corrected him. "See? Here's a plain white one like the master chefs wear." I tied it on him. It came to the floor.

"Now," I continued, "does your mom buy cake mixes?"

"Yup," said Buddy.

"Where does she keep them?"

Buddy pointed to a cupboard. I opened it and looked inside. I found flour, sugar, baking powder, boxes of cake and frosting mix, and (thank goodness) way in the back of the cupboard, two boxes of E-Z-Bake Brownee Mix. (Why can't food companies spell things properly?)

"Here we go!" I said. I decided we'd better make both boxes, a double batch, since there would be fourteen people at the picnic. Mrs Barrett would probably appreciate the leftovers.

Buddy and I looked at the instructions on the back of the box.

"What do we need to add to the mix?" I asked him.

He frowned. "An egg and . . . and some o-*oil*," he finally pronounced triumphantly.

"Good. OK, you get out the eggs and the bottle of oil, and I'll get the pans and mixing bowls."

"What should I do?" asked Suzi.

"You can, um, get some dish towels," I replied. They were the first unbreakable things that came to mind. Luckily, she didn't ask me what they were for. I didn't know at the time, but I figured we'd use them for something.

I was right. We needed the towels when Buddy dropped an egg on the floor, and again when Suzi turned on the electric mixer just as Buddy was lowering the beaters into the batter.

The brownies finally went into the oven at twelve thirty-five. They had to bake for a half an hour. We would only be five or ten minutes late to the picnic.

We spent that half hour cleaning the chocolate batter off the wall around the mixer, and washing the bowls and spoons. At five past one I removed the pans from the oven and tested the brownies with a knife. They were done. And they smelled divine!

I remembered just in time that you're not supposed to cut brownies into squares before they're cool, so I carried the pans over to the Pikes' with oven gloves. I had to make two trips: the first with one batch of brownies, Pow, and the Barrett kids (Suzi took our sandwiches), the second with the other batch after the Barretts had been left at the Pikes'.

The Pikes' back garden looked festive but crowded. Claudia and Stacey had spread blankets on the ground and laid out paper plates, cups, and napkins, and plastic spoons and forks. The Pike kids had been busy decorating the yard with flags and balloons left over from a recent birthday party.

I took a quick head count to make sure we were all accounted for, and came up with fifteen.

"Hey, Stacey," I said. "Come here."

"What is it?" Stacey trotted over to me, looking as fabulous as always. She was wearing a simple pink T-shirt under a baggy jumpsuit with big pink and red flowers all over it. Her shiny hair bounced over her shoulders. I was wearing blue jean shorts and a white T-shirt that said GENIUS INSIDE. I looked ordinary next to Stacey.

"How many Pike kids are there?" I asked.

"Eight," Stacey replied. "You know that."

"Right, and there are three Barrett kids. That makes eleven. Plus you and Claudia and me – fourteen."

"Yeah?"

"Now count the people in the yard."

Stacey counted. ". . . thirteen, fourteen, fifteen. . . *Fifteen?*"

"That's what I just realized," I said.

"Well, let's see who doesn't belong here."

"All right," I replied. "There are Buddy, Suzi and Marnie."

"And there are Mallory, Byron, Adam, Jordan, Vanessa, Nicky, Margo, Claire and Jenny."

"You just counted nine Pikes," I informed Stacey.

"Jenny!" cried Stacey. "What's Jenny Prezzioso doing here?"

"Oh," I groaned. Jenny the brat. She lived right around the corner. "I wonder why we didn't notice her earlier." Jenny was the only kid in the garden who appeared to be dressed for a wedding. She had on a pink pinafore over a spotless white dress, white tights, and pink Mary Janes. Her mother had plaited her hair and tied pink ribbons at the ends.

Claudia was carrying food out of the house and setting it on the blankets. The picnic was almost ready. "We might as well ask Jenny to stay," said Stacey.

I made a face, but said, "I guess you're right."

"I'll go inside and call Mrs Prezzioso," Stacey offered. She returned a few minutes later saying, "It's OK."

Claudia and Stacey and I settled the kids on

the blankets. We passed out sandwiches and poured cups of lemonade and milk. For two and a half minutes, the twelve children were as good as gold. Then something very small happened. Jordan put his sandwich down, turned to Nicky, aimed his index fingers at him, and went, "Bzzz."

The result was astonishing. Nicky yelped and said, "Claudia, Jordan gave me the Bizzer Sign!"

"What's the Bizzer Sign?" I whispered to Stacey.

"Something the Pike kids made up. It's like an insult or something. They use it when they want to annoy each other. Or their friends."

"Ignore him," Claudia told Nicky.

"But he gave me the *Bizzer Sign!*"

"*Ignore* him."

"But he *gave me the Bizzer Sign!*"

Claudia sighed. She glanced at Stacey and me. I shrugged.

The next thing we knew, Adam was giving Jenny the Bizzer Sign, and Buddy was giving Suzi the Bizzer Sign.

Both Jenny and Suzi began to cry.

Then Mallory, who is usually quite well behaved, gave Byron the Bizzer Sign, and *he* began to cry.

Within the next thirty seconds, seven kids were crying and seven were bizzing and grinning. (Marnie was making the ham face.)

This may be how a war gets started. One day, a world leader pokes another world leader in the ribs and says, "Nyah, nyah, nyah." The second world leader begins to cry, and suddenly their countries are fighting each other.

Our picnic had gone from a dream to a disaster in under five minutes.

Luckily, I had a brainstorm. In the midst of the pandemonium, I stood up and shouted, "Who wants brownies?"

"I do!" shouted every single kid, except Marnie.

"Great," I said, "but you can't have any until you stop teasing each other, finish your sandwiches, and behave yourselves. And the next person who gives somebody the Bizzer Sign will have to go inside."

Silence reigned. Then laughter. Then some elephant jokes. Fifteen minutes later, the sandwiches were gone and I was passing around brownies. I broke off a piece of one and handed it to Marnie, wondering whether she would eat it.

"Hey!" shouted Mallory. "Don't give her that!"

She dived over Vanessa and Buddy and snatched the brownie out of Marnie's fist.

"What do you think you're doing?" I said crossly. "You'll get a brownie in a minute, Mallory."

Mallory looked at me with wounded eyes. "She's allergic," she said quietly. "Marnie can't eat chocolate. She'll get sick."

"Are you sure?" I exclaimed. "Mrs Barrett never told me that."

"I'm positive. You can ask my mom."

I apologized to Mallory four times. Then I began to feel angry. The Barrett kids were great and they needed me, but their mother was a problem. She never gave me instructions. She hardly paid any attention to her children. She was totally disorganized. Plus, I was doing all her housework, and she was only paying me regular babysitting wages.

I planned to talk to Mrs Barrett about every single one of my grievances, but when she blew through the front door late that afternoon, her perfume trailing behind her, she started praising me right away. She looked around at the tidy house, the tidy children, and the plate of leftover brownies, and said, "Dawn, I swear, you're a wonder. I don't know how you do it.

Thank you so much. Mrs Pike said you were a real find, and she was right."

What could I say? All my complaints flew out of my head. So I kissed the kids goodbye and left.

Chapter 9

Wednesday, May 20

This evning I babysat for Dawn Shafers brother Jeff. I could tell he thoght he was to old for a babysitter but Dawn was sitting at the Barretts and her mom had suddenly got tickits to a concert and Mrs Shaffer. didn't want to leave Jeff alone at night. She called me at the last minute and luckily I was free. Sitting for Jeff was an easy job.

But! Dawn I noticed this is the second night in a row you've sat at the Baretts. And I looked in our apontment book and you were their four times last week. Maybe you are overdoing it?

I am telling you this as a freind.

And I listened to Claudia as a friend. I knew she wasn't jealous because I had so many sitting jobs. The truth was that I was practically living at the Barretts'. Mrs Barrett constantly needed someone to watch the kids, and she constantly called me. A couple of times I hadn't been available, so Kristy or Mary Anne had gone, but Mrs Barrett said the children, especially Buddy, liked me best.

It was flattering – but I was so busy! Once I had even missed a meeting of the Babysitters Club. Mrs Barrett had promised me she would be home by five thirty, and she didn't get back until five past six. If she'd been somewhere important, say at a job interview, I wouldn't have minded so much. But she'd just been out shopping with a friend.

On the Monday after the picnic at the Pikes', I finally asked Mrs Barrett about Marnie's chocolate allergy. I waited until she'd returned for the evening, so she couldn't rush off.

After she'd paid me, I said, "Mrs Barrett, could I talk to you for a sec?"

Something passed over her eyes then. It was a look – just the briefest look – of fear? Annoyance? I couldn't tell.

Anyway, we sat down in the living room and before I could lose my nerve, I said, "How come you didn't tell me Marnie's allergic to chocolate?"

"Oh, dear," said Mrs Barrett. Sitting cross-legged on the couch in her beautifully tailored suit, she looked chic and fashionable and oh-so-put-together – from the neck down. From the neck up, she looked weary and worried. There were lines around her eyes and at the corners of her mouth, and I caught sight of a few grey hairs. But I knew that she was only thirty-three years old.

She rubbed her eyes tiredly. "I didn't tell you about Marnie's allergy?"

"No," I replied. "And I almost gave her a piece of brownie the other day. Mallory Pike stopped me just in time."

"Thank goodness," said Mrs Barrett. And then she added, "Poor baby" as Marnie toddled into the living room and held her arms out to be picked up. Mrs Barrett pulled her into her lap and rocked her back and forth.

"Does she have any other allergies?" I asked.

"Not that we know of." Mrs Barrett kissed the top of Marnie's head.

"What about Buddy and Suzi? I mean, is there anything else I should know?"

Mrs Barrett's face softened and I thought I was going to hear all about nightmares and childish fears and favourite foods. Then it hardened again, and she said crisply, "Just one thing. If my ex-husband ever calls, don't let him talk to the children, don't tell him he can see the children, and don't tell him I'm out. Say you're a mother's helper and I'm busy."

Mrs Barrett looked as if she was going to say more, but a crash sounded in the playroom, followed by a shriek from Suzi.

"Uh-oh," said Mrs Barrett. She hoisted Marnie on to her hip and hurried into the playroom. I followed.

A horrible sight met our eyes. When we had left Buddy and Suzi, they'd been watching a rerun of *The Brady Bunch* on TV. But while Mrs Barrett and I had been in the living room, they had transformed the playroom into a disaster area. A bowl of water sat in the middle of the floor, surrounded by half-full paper cups and jars – and bottles of food colouring. They had been experimenting with the colours, but it had got out of hand. Little puddles of pink and blue and yellow water were everywhere. The kids' clothes were streaked, and several stuffed animals now had greenish fur. The shriek had occurred when Buddy had spilled pink water over Suzi's head.

He said it was an accident.

Suzi disagreed.

Mrs Barrett looked ready to fall apart. She hugged Marnie to her and closed her eyes. I thought she might even cry. Since my mother is a big crier, I know the signs well.

"I'll take care of it," I told Mrs Barrett. "Why don't you dry Suzi off? Buddy, go get the paper towels. We'll clean up."

"How come Suzi doesn't have to clean up?" whined Buddy. "She made a mess, too."

"I know, but she's all wet. Besides, if you get the towels, I'll show you a trick."

Buddy hesitated for just a second. "OK!" he agreed.

Mrs Barrett took the girls upstairs, and Buddy returned with the towels. I placed one square over a puddle, soaked it up, and then held the towel out for Buddy to see.

"It's pink!" he exclaimed. "Let me try!" So Buddy went around wiping up puddles, and I emptied the jars and cups into the bowl and returned everything to the sink in the kitchen. Then I scrubbed at the stuffed animals, but even after several minutes they still had a greenish cast to them.

Buddy finished with the puddles and we hung several of the colourful paper towels up as artwork.

Then Mrs Barrett returned with Marnie and a smiling Suzi, and peeped into the playroom.

"Oh, thank goodness, Dawn," she said. "It looks wonderful in there. I don't know what I'd do without you." She began to usher me towards the front door. As I put my sweatshirt on, she handed me an extra tip. "For averting a crisis," she explained. "You're a lifesaver. Each time you sit, the house looks better when you leave than it did when you arrived. I used to be such an organized person, but since the divorce, everything seems overwhelming. Money is a little tight, too. If the children's father would— Oh, well. Anyway, I hope you know how much I appreciate you. I think you're the glue that's holding us together."

The glue that was holding them together? That was a little scary. It sounded like an awfully big responsibility.

At that moment, the phone rang. "I'll get it!" Mrs Barrett yelled, but she was too late. We could already hear Buddy on the extension in the kitchen saying, "Hello?"

"Buddy, I told you, you are not to answer the phone!" Mrs Barrett shouted.

"It's Dad, Mom," Buddy shouted back.

Mrs Barrett clenched her teeth.

"He says where are we? He says you were supposed to drop Suzi and me off at his apartment by five-thirty, and he's been waiting for half an hour."

"Oh-my-goodness-I-completely-forgot!" Mrs Barrett exclaimed. "Dawn, I'll see you on Wednesday afternoon, right?"

"Right," I replied. "At three o'clock." But Mrs Barrett didn't even hear my last words. She was already rushing for the phone.

Over the next couple of weeks, I babysat for the Barretts an awful lot. This did not escape any member of the club. They didn't mind, of course, except when it cut into meetings.

But I minded a few things. Mrs Barrett's disorganization caused a number of problems. One afternoon when I was sitting, Suzi said she didn't feel well – and immediately threw up all over the kitchen floor. I cleaned up the mess, then held my hand to her forehead and realized she had a fever.

I dialled the number Mrs Barrett had left by the phone. It was for an employment agency where she had found a temporary afternoon job.

The gruff voice that answered the phone said, "Hurley's Garage."

Hurley's Garage? "I guess you don't have a Mrs Barrett working there, do you?" I asked.

"Sorry, kid," replied the man.

"Great," I said to no one in particular as I hung up the phone. "Mrs Barrett left the wrong number."

At that moment, Suzi threw up again.

As I cleaned up the second mess, I racked my brain trying to remember whether Mrs Barrett had mentioned the name of the agency where she was working. I didn't think she had.

Just in case, I opened the yellow pages of the phone book and scanned the firms listed under EMPLOYMENT AGENCIES, but nothing sounded familiar. Then Suzi began to gag again. That time I managed to rush her to the kitchen sink before she got sick.

I put Marnie in her playpen, sent Buddy over to the Pikes', rolled up the rug in the bathroom, and spent the rest of the afternoon there with Suzi, reading to her, and holding her head over the toilet every time she had to throw up.

She was miserable. I was angry at her mother.

When Mrs Barrett came home, I told her, rather crossly, about the mixed-up phone number. She apologized, but it was a little late for that. If Suzi hadn't needed her so badly, I might have said more to her.

Two days later, I came down with Suzi's bug and spent hours in the bathroom. Mom and Jeff caught the bug from me, and the Pike kids caught it from Buddy, who had been spreading it around the afternoon I sent him to their house while I was taking care of Suzi.

Another day, as Mrs Barrett rushed out of the door, Buddy called plaintively after her, "Hey, Mom, my homework. . ."

"I'll look at it tonight," she called to him, and continued down the walk.

Buddy burst into tears and ran to his room.

I ran after him, pausing in his doorway. "Hey, old Buddy. What's the matter? Can I come in?"

He was lying face down on his bed, but I saw him nod his head.

I sat next to him and patted his back. "Can you tell me what's wrong?" I asked.

He hiccupped. "My homework."

"Do you need help with it?"

"I need *Mom's* help." He rolled over and looked at me mournfully.

"Are you sure I won't do? I'm pretty smart," I told him. "I'm in seventh grade."

Buddy managed a smile. "It's not that. We're

studying families. We're supposed to make a family tree tonight, starting with our grandparents. You won't know their names. *I* don't know them. They're just Gram and Gramps and Gee-ma and Gee-pa. And I have to bring it to school *tomorrow* and it's our first homework ever and I want it to be good."

"Oh, I see."

"And Mom said she'd help," Buddy moaned, "but she won't. Not really. She's always too tired at night to do anything."

"Well, let's make it easy on her," I suggested. "Why don't we make the tree part, and then she can tell you the names to fill in. Do you know how many aunts and uncles you have?"

Buddy nodded uncertainly.

So I busied the girls with some toys, and then Buddy and I set to work. It took a lot of questioning and two phone calls to Mrs Pike, but we finally figured out where the Barrett relatives belonged on the tree. Then I showed Buddy how to make boxes and lines and spaces. When he was finished, he had a beautiful blank tree. I just hoped it was accurate. If it wasn't, he'd have a lot of erasing to do.

A week later, Buddy showed up at my house after school. He'd never done that before. When I opened the door, he didn't say a word – just held out a large piece of paper. It was his completed family tree. A gold star was glued to the top.

"My teacher loved it," he told me. "Thanks for helping me, Dawn."

"You're welcome, Buddy," I replied, and gave him a hug. But all the while, I was thinking that Mrs Barrett should be hugging Buddy for his good work.

Chapter 10

Thursday, May 21st

This afternoon I babysat for David Michael. Poor kid. I bet it's hard being the youngest in a big family. Kristy, Sam and Charlie were all off doing other things, and Mrs Thomas was at work, of course. So that left David Michael.

When I came over, he looked kind of sad. As soon as Kristy left the house, he said, "Stacey, let's have a snack and a talk." Little kids today have a lot to worry about.

You guys should know that David Michael is getting very worried about moving into Watson's house. That was why he wanted to talk to me. Because I moved recently. It turns out that he watched the men unloading our furniture from the van last August. He saw them drop a lamp and break it. And he saw something or other covered with a drop cloth that looked like a ghost to him. He's pretty scared, all right.

Apparently, David Michael was more interested in talking than in snacking. Stacey fixed him a plate of crackers and peanut butter and poured him a glass of juice, but he hardly looked at the food.

"Stacey," he said, "when you moved, did the men pack up *every*thing in the van?"

"Oh, yes," she said reassuringly. "Every last thing. Nothing was left behind."

"Are you sure?"

"Positive."

David Michael began to look tearful. "Do you have any pets?" he asked.

"No," Stacey replied, puzzled. Then suddenly she caught on. "Oh, David Michael," she cried.

"They won't put *Louie* in the van. Dogs don't go in vans."

"I hope not. Louie doesn't like dark places."

"Anyway, you're only moving across town. Your mom will drive Louie to Watson's house in the car. Louie likes car rides, doesn't he?"

David Michael brightened. "He loves them!"

"Has he ever been to Watson's house?"

David Michael nodded. "A few times."

"See? He'll even know where he's going. No big deal."

A pause. Then, "Stacey, moving vans sometimes have accidents."

"They do?" Stacey said, wondering what David Michael was getting at now.

"Yesterday I saw a TV show where this van was driving along a mountain road and suddenly it had an accident and it skidded and went *shwooo*" (David Michael demonstrated the van sailing over a cliff.) "down the mountain and the doors flew open and things fell out and a man found the accident and saw a teddy bear on the ground all squashed and ripped. Also a tricycle with the wheels bent."

"But, David Michael, there are no mountains here in Stoneybrook. It'll only take a few minutes to drive from Bradford Court to Watson's house.

Anyway, our moving van travelled from New York City to Stoneybrook with no problems at all—"

"The lamp broke."

"—and Dawn Schafer's moving van travelled from California to Connecticut without any trouble. That's three thousand miles. . . I *know* our lamp got broken. So did a vase. But moving men aren't perfect."

"Well, I don't want them moving my space station."

"I bet if you tell your mom that, she'll take it to Watson's in the car sometime. Or Charlie will. He'll be able to drive by then."

David Michael nodded. He bit an infinitesimally small corner off of one of the crackers. Stacey had the feeling that the moving van wasn't *really* what was worrying him. She waited patiently.

David Michael returned the rest of the cracker to the plate, then let loose with a barrage of nervous questions. "When we move to Watson's, who will be my friends? Where will I go to school? Will I still see Patrick and Frankie?" (Current friends.) "Where will I sleep? Where will my mom sleep? Where will Louie sleep? What if Louie tries to come back to his old house?" The questions went on and on.

Stacey did her best to answer them, but she didn't think David Michael would stop worrying about the move until it was over.

She mentioned that to Kristy at the next meeting of the Babysitters Club. "That's a long time for a little kid to worry," Stacey pointed out. "It'll be three or four months before you move."

"Inobutthdobawt." Kristy had three pieces of toffee in her mouth. Claudia, the junk food junkie, had been sent a box of it by her aunt and uncle who were visiting Atlantic City in New Jersey. She had hidden the candy in her room, along with her Kit Kats and Rolos and M&Ms, and had handed around pieces at the beginning of the meeting. We all had gooey mouthfuls of the stuff, except for Stacey, who's diabetic and can't eat most sweets.

Stacey giggled. "What?" she asked Kristy.

Kristy swallowed several times. "I know," she said at last, "but there's nothing we can do about it. Mom and Watson aren't getting married until the end of September. Mom knows David Michael is scared, so they talk about the move sometimes. A little too often, in my opinion."

"What do you mean?" I asked.

"Well, I don't want to hear about the move day in and day out. I'm not thrilled with the idea,

104

either – but for different reasons."

Mary Anne looked solemnly out of the window. "I can't believe you won't be next door to me any more," she told Kristy. "All my life, when I've looked out of my side bedroom window, I've looked into yours."

"Yeah," said Kristy huskily. "Me, too."

Before things got too sad, I said, "Well, when you look out of your new bedroom window, Kristy, you'll look right into Morbidda Destiny's."

Everyone laughed.

"You know," said Kristy, "we've been saying that a move across town is really no big deal. I'll still go to Stoneybrook Middle School, and we'll still be friends and all that. But what are we going to do about the meetings of the Babysitters Club? And how am I supposed to sit for Jamie Newton and the Pikes and everyone? No one's going to want to drive all the way to Watson's to pick me up, when you guys are right here and can walk to our clients."

We chewed in thoughtful silence. We must have looked like we were at a funeral.

After a while Claudia spoke up. "Maybe it won't be so bad. You'll get new clients, Kristy. You'll have a whole new neighbourhood full of kids to yourself. When you can't handle the jobs, we'll go. Your move will expand our club. We'll be babysitting all over town!"

Claudia's excitement was contagious. She and Mary Anne and Kristy and I reached for more toffee. Stacey reached for a soda cracker.

"But the meetings," said Kristy, looking downcast again. "Who's going to drive me to Bradford Court three times a week?"

No one could answer her question. I began to have a funny feeling in the pit of my stomach.

"Can't you ride your bike over?" asked Stacey. "I know it's a few miles, but you don't mind a little exercise, do you?"

"Of course not," Kristy answered. "I love to ride my bike. But Mom won't let me ride from Watson's to Bradford Court."

"How come?" I asked. "She lets you ride downtown and stuff."

"Only with a friend. Safety in numbers and all that," said Kristy.

"Oh."

"I mean, she's not strict, but she *is* careful. Even Mom has her limits. Besides, let's say Mom gave me permission to ride across town alone. OK. It takes about a half an hour each way when you figure in stopping at lights and running into rush-hour traffic. That means I'd have to leave

Watson's at five o'clock for a five-thirty meeting, and I wouldn't get home until six-thirty. In the winter, it would be pitch-black by then."

The problem was looking bigger and bigger.

"Hey, you guys," said Claudia suddenly. "We're not thinking. We're assuming we have to go on holding the meetings in my room, but who says so? Just because we've held them here since the beginning doesn't mean it's the only place for them."

"Then our clients wouldn't know where to reach us," I said.

"Oh, right." Kristy, who had just started to look hopeful, dropped her hands into her lap. "Stupid, stupid Watson," she muttered.

"Hey, Kristy, don't get down on Watson," I said gently. "It's not his fault. It's not anybody's fault."

"A lot *you* know." Kristy didn't even bother to look at me.

"I may know more than you think," I said quietly. "You're not the only one whose parents got divorced."

"No, but I'm the only one whose mother chose to get married to a jerk who's so rich he lives three and a half miles away on Millionaire's Lane, which is what they should call that gross street he can afford to live on. And I'm the only one who may have to drop out of the club. The club *I* started."

"Oh, Kristy!" I exclaimed, forgetting her jab at me. "You can't drop out of the club!"

"No. We won't let you," said Mary Anne staunchly. "We couldn't run your club without you. It wouldn't be right."

"Yeah," said Claudia. "No Kristy, no club."

Then we all looked at each other with the awful realization of what Claudia's words might mean.

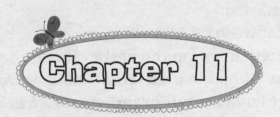

Chapter 11

The next day was the beginning of Memorial Day weekend. The Stoneybrook schools were closed on Monday. In California, we usually spent most of the long weekend at the beach. There was no chance of that in Connecticut. Although we lived near the coast and the weather was beautiful, the temperature had dropped back to about twenty degrees. Mary Anne assured me that was normal. I didn't care. On Saturday morning, I shouted at my clock radio and called the weatherman a cheesebrain. (Several days earlier, I'd called him a magician and a saint.)

When I heard that the ocean temperature (the *Atlantic* Ocean temperature, that is) was ten degrees, I called the weatherman a moron.

Nevertheless, my mother, who was giving a picnic on Saturday, decided to hold it outdoors. I told her it was probably going to be the first picnic ever attended by people wearing down jackets.

Mom just rolled her eyes heavenward and said, "For pity's sake, Dawn. It's perfectly pleasant outside."

No, it wasn't.

I tried to be enthusiastic about the picnic anyway. It had started off as just a small party for my mom and grandparents, but it had grown. First, Mom had invited Mr Spier and Mary Anne. Then I had asked if I could invite the Thomases, the Kishis, and the McGills. Then Jeff had asked if we could invite the Pikes, and finally I decided to ask the Barretts and (out of guilt) the Prezziosos.

Most of them couldn't come, since they already had plans. In fact, apart from my grandparents and the Spiers, the only people who were able to attend were the Barretts, and Kristy and David Michael. (Mrs Thomas was giving a party for her relatives and Watson and his kids on Saturday night, so she'd be busy getting ready for it during the day, but Kristy said she wanted to come to our picnic anyway. I was very flattered.)

On Saturday morning, shivering in a sweatshirt and blue jeans, I helped Mom set up a table and our lawn furniture in the back garden. Then, while Jeff hosed everything down (the furniture was dusty from sitting in the barn) and decorated the garden with balloons, flags, crepe paper, and lanterns, Mom and I worked on the food.

"You know, Mom," I said, surveying the messy kitchen, "some people don't like tofu."

"Really?" she replied vaguely.

"And, Mom, before the guests arrive this afternoon, could you find matching socks? Mr Spier would probably really appreciate it if your socks matched. And your earrings."

"My earrings? I know *they* match, honey. I just put them on. . . I wonder if I could substitute raw honey for sugar in this recipe."

"They don't match, Mom. They're both gold hoops, but they're different sizes. Here, let me look at that recipe." I was beginning to feel nervous.

"I've got a great idea," I said on impulse. "Instead of trying to make this fancy stuff, why don't we go to the grocery store, buy hamburger patties, hot dogs, buns and potato salad, and serve that? Grandpa can barbecue. We won't have to cook at all."

"*Red meat?*" exclaimed my mother. "*Hot dogs?* Do you know what's in a hot dog?"

"Yes, and I don't even want to think about it. I'd rather eat tofu any day. But we're in *Connecticut*. In Connecticut, people barbecue things. Especially at picnics. Don't you think we should serve food our guests will like?" I tried to imagine Kristy looking at a table of dried fruit, tofu salads and raw vegetables. She'd go hungry before she'd touch a thing.

"I suppose," said Mom. I could tell that the idea of not having to cook was very appealing to her. "Do you really think we can buy ready-made potato salad?"

"Sure. In the deli section at the grocery. I've seen it. Vats of it. We could probably buy ready-made green salad, too. It might be a little expensive, but we won't have to prepare anything."

Mom considered this for all of two seconds. "Let's go!" she cried. "What a relief!"

We made a dash for the car. On the way to the shopping centre, I realized we didn't have a grill, so we had to buy one of those, too. It was a costly morning, but it was worth it.

As we were driving back home, the car loaded down with food and a big red Weber grill, I said casually, "Hey, Mom, I thought when you were in high school your parents didn't approve of Mary Anne's father."

"That's right, sweetie."

"Well, what's going to happen when they see each other today?"

112

"Oh, nothing. That was years ago," Mom answered mildly.

But I thought she looked uncomfortable.

Our guests were invited for one-fifteen. In California, one o'clock means two or two-thirty. Here in Connecticut, every last guest had arrived by one-fifteen. Luckily, since we didn't have much to do except start the Weber grill, we were ready anyway. The back garden was decorated and the furniture was clean. All we had to do was carry out the food.

When that was done, I pulled Kristy and Mary Anne aside so we could survey the scene. Jeff, David Michael, Buddy and Suzi were playing ball. Mrs Barrett was bouncing Marnie on her knees and talking to my grandmother. My grandfather was lighting the fire in the grill. And Mom and Mr Spier were sitting as close together as they could possibly sit, their heads bent in quiet laughter.

"Keep an eye on them," I said to my friends. "This is a good opportunity to see how they're acting with each other these days. And keep an eye on my grandparents and your father, Mary Anne. It could be interesting. We may have to – to avert a crisis," I said, remembering words Mrs Barrett had once used.

"OK," whispered Mary Anne.

"Hey," Kristy exclaimed, looking awed. "Mary Anne, where are your father's glasses?"

"He got contacts," Mary Anne replied.

"Your *father*?"

Mary Anne nodded.

"Got *contacts*?"

"Yup."

I began to giggle.

"I don't believe it. I absolutely do not believe it," said Kristy. "It's amazing. Get me a chair, somebody. I may have to sit down."

Mary Anne made a great show of pulling up a lawn chair, and Kristy made a great show of collapsing into it with one hand pressed over her heart.

When we calmed down, I dragged a garden chair next to Kristy's chair and Mary Anne and I both sat in it. Then the three of us watched the adults.

It didn't take me long to realize that my grandmother was only pretending to have a conversation with Mrs Barrett. All she did was ask questions that required long answers, and while Mrs Barrett was talking, Granny would keep shooting little glances over at Mom and Mr Spier.

Pop-Pop (my grandfather) was watching them, too. Once he got the fire started, there wasn't much for him to do until the coals were hot. Even so, he stood over the grill, occasionally poking a lump of charcoal, but mostly just gazing at the lovebirds.

Lovebirds. That's exactly what they looked like. If one of them had cooed – even Mr Spier – I wouldn't have been the least bit surprised.

I tried to read the expression on Pop-Pop's face. He didn't look angry. I nudged Mary Anne and then Kristy. "How would you say my grandfather looks?" I asked them.

"Well, he looks very nice," replied Kristy. "This is the first time I've ever met him, of course, but I'd say he looks good, although his shirt doesn't exactly match his trousers."

"No!" I exclaimed. "I mean, what does he look like he's thinking about as he watches my mom and Mary Anne's dad? Mary Anne, what do you think?"

"I don't know, I can't tell."

"Do you think he looks like he disapproves?"

"No," answered Mary Anne and Kristy.

"Do you think he looks deliriously happy?"

"No," they replied.

"Deliriously proud?"

"No."

We weren't getting anywhere.

"What about Granny?" I asked. "She's been watching them the whole time she's been talking to Mrs Barrett."

"It's hard to tell," said Mary Anne. "If you want my honest opinion, she has to pretend she's interested in what Mrs Barrett is saying, and there's no room on her face for any other expression."

Adults certainly are hard to understand. Sometimes they seem to have several faces. It's as if they own masks, and you *know* they own masks, but you can't always tell their masks from their real expressions. Why do they make everything so complicated?

The picnic became more interesting when we started eating. Mom settled the little kids – Jeff, David Michael, Buddy and Suzi – at a child-size picnic table. Then she arranged Marnie and the adults – who were going to eat on their laps – in a semicircle of lawn chairs. She left Mary Anne and Kristy and me on our own, so we just inconspicuously tacked ourselves on to one end of the semicircle. From there we had a bird's-eye view of the adults.

The first interesting thing that happened

was that Pop-Pop sat himself down next to Mr Spier and said, "So, Richard, how are things at Thompson, Thompson, and Abrams?"

"Oh," replied Mary Anne's father, "I haven't been with them in quite some time."

"Oh?"

"No, I started my own firm about four years ago. I practise in Stamford."

"Oh?"

"Yes. It's doing very well, too. Leaving Thompson's was the best decision I ever made."

"Oh?"

(It's amazing how many meanings the word *oh* seems to have. Mr Spier's *oh* had sounded surprised. Pop-Pop's first *oh* had sounded suspicious. His second *oh* had sounded impressed. His third *oh* had sounded sort of awed.)

Mary Anne and I glanced at each other. *That* conversation seemed to have gone all right.

A little while later, Granny leaned over and said, "Richard, are you still living on Taylor Street?" (Taylor Street is the neighbourhood Mr Spier had grown up in.)

"Why, no," he replied. "We live on Bradford Court. Mary Anne's mother and I moved out of the house on Taylor Street several months before Mary Anne was born."

Again Mr Spier sounded surprised. He was probably wondering why my grandparents didn't know all this stuff. The truth is, Mom and her parents rarely discuss Touchy Subjects. And their three Touchiest Subjects at that time were the divorce, my father, and Mary Anne's father. I was beginning to think that Mom had brought Granny, Pop-Pop, and Mr Spier together just so that my grandparents could see how well Mary Anne's father had done for himself, not to mention the fact that he's a perfectly nice, normal guy.

Towards the end of the meal, Pop-Pop got into a discussion of banking laws with Mr Spier. (Pop-Pop is a banker.) The talk went on and on. Sometimes they seemed to be arguing, but at the same time enjoying themselves. The rest of the time they were agreeing with each other and talking earnestly.

Mom looked so happy about that that she relaxed and became involved in a conversation with Granny and Mrs Barrett.

Kristy and Mary Anne and I, satisfied that things were going well, snuck over to the barn where Kristy and I took turns swinging through the loft on the rope, while Mary Anne sat outside on a bale of hay and daydreamed.

Later, as the guests were leaving, Mrs Barrett

asked if I could babysit after school on Tuesday. I was busy, but Mary Anne was free, so she took the job.

I decided that it had been a good day all around, even if it had been chilly. I went to bed that night and had a lovely dream in which Mom and Mr Spier got married and Mary Anne and I were in the wedding. It was a beautiful ceremony, except that the bride and groom were wearing ski jackets and snow pants.

Chapter 12

Tuesday, May 26th

This afternoon I babysat for Buddy, Suzi and Marnie Barrett. What a time I had! I don't know if it's the weather or problems with the divorce or what, but the kids were wild. Wild and cranky. I'm sure the sitter they really wanted was Dawn. I don't know how you handle them, Dawn. I hope they behave better for you than they do for me.

By the way, there was a really strange phone call from Mr Barrett today, wanting to know where Buddy was. I wouldn't give him any information. When I told

Mrs Barrett about the call, she turned purple (not really) and said he shouldn't have called here when he knew darn well she'd be out. What's going on? I think we should all be careful of calls from Mr Barrett.

When Mary Anne got home from the Barretts' that afternoon, the first thing she did was call me. She was extremely miffed.

"Dawn," she exclaimed, "how can you possibly sit at the Barretts' so often?"

"What do you mean?" I asked.

"What do I *mean*?! They're terrors, that's what I mean! If I were their mother, I'd have . . . I don't know what I'd have done, but I'd have done something by now. Something drastic."

"You've sat for them before," I pointed out.

Mary Anne calmed down somewhat. "I know, and they were a little wild then, but nothing like today."

"Maybe it was the weather." It had been raining for three days.

"Maybe. That must have been part of it, but

you always get along so well with them. They really like you. It's almost as if you have – what do you call it? – some kind of chemistry with them. I don't think we have any chemistry at all."

"They do like me," I admitted. Lately Buddy had come over to our house more and more often, and since Suzi had learned how to use the phone, she had started calling me, although she never had much to say. "What did they do today?" I asked Mary Anne.

"What *didn't* they do?" she replied. She began to describe the afternoon. The first part of it sounded very familiar. When Mary Anne rang the bell, Buddy, Suzi and Pow had answered the door. Buddy was wearing the cowboy hat and swimming flippers and was aiming his ray gun at Mary Anne.

He greeted her with a, "Fshoo, fshoo. Bzzzzt," followed by a gleeful, "I got you! You're dead! You're completely dead!"

Although Mary Anne didn't mention anything about not using guns, she did say, "Well, I'm not dead for long, because I'm coming into your house. Stand aside, Martian man."

"*Mar*tian man?! I'm not a Martian man. I'm a cowboy from Venus. And this is my Venus weapon." Buddy jumped into a position of offence, legs spread, arms extended, holding the ray gun stiffly. He aimed it first at Mary Anne, then at Pow. But suddenly he dropped the gun and gave Suzi the Bizzer Sign instead.

Suzi burst into tears.

Marnie, sitting alone in her high chair in the kitchen (wearing only a nappy), burst into tears, too. (Sometimes tears are contagious.)

"Hi, Mary Anne!" called Mrs Barrett as she rushed downstairs. She ignored the crying children, frantically threw on her raincoat, and as usual, ran out of the door without giving the babysitter any instructions. Mary Anne did, however, hear her call, "Don't forget that Marnie's allergic to chocolate!" as she got into her car.

"Great," muttered Mary Anne, closing the front door.

Mrs Barrett wasn't going on an interview that afternoon. She was just running errands and wanted to do them by herself. Mary Anne could see why.

In order to get the kids under control, Mary Anne sent Buddy outside to walk Pow. He asked if he could wear the flippers, and Mary Anne said yes, since she thought the walk would take longer that way.

Then she gave Suzi a cracker and told her to

go try to find *Sesame Street* on TV. Suzi stopped crying right away. With Suzi and Buddy occupied, Mary Anne turned her attention to Marnie.

"OK, Marnie-o," she said, lifting her out of the high chair. "First we'll get you cleaned up, then we'll get you a fresh nappy, and then we'll get you dressed."

"No-no," said Marnie.

"Yes-yes," said Mary Anne.

Marnie screamed while Mary Anne wiped her face, changed her nappy, and dressed her. Then suddenly she stopped crying. Mary Anne held her up to a mirror and said, "Pretty!"

Marnie made the ham face. She was back to her usual sunny self.

Mary Anne was just carrying Marnie downstairs when Buddy returned with Pow. He took Pow's leash off, hung it in the kitchen, patted the dog affectionately, ran into the playroom, and gave Suzi the Bizzer Sign.

Suzi burst into tears.

Marnie burst into tears.

Mary Anne was back where she started. "Buddy," she said, "you give one more Bizzer Sign to anyone today – *anyone* – and you'll have to stay in your room until your mother comes home."

"No, I won't."

"Yes, you will. I'm in charge here and what I say goes."

"Will you tell my mom if I'm bad?"

"I might."

"Tell tale."

Mary Anne shrugged her shoulders. "That's the way it is." She turned to Suzi and Marnie. "OK, you guys, quieten down. You know what we're going to do today?"

"Not read," said Buddy.

"Not colour," said Suzi.

"Not watch TV," said Buddy.

"Not play Monopoly," said Suzi.

"Nope," replied Mary Anne. "I can tell you're tired of the same old rainy-day stuff. Today we're going to go outdoors for a puddle walk, and then we're going to come back inside and go camping and have a picnic."

"*Really?*" cried Buddy.

"Yes," answered Mary Anne. "Now, to take a puddle walk, the first thing you guys have to do is find your bathing suits. Do you know where they are?"

"Yes, yes!" shouted Buddy and Suzi, jumping up and down.

Marnie tried to jump up and down, too, but

all she could do was bend her knees and make the ham face.

"OK, upstairs and into your suits."

"Even Marnie?" asked Suzi.

"What about you?" Buddy wanted to know. "Did you bring your suit?"

"No, but it doesn't matter. Marnie and I won't really need them. Go upstairs and change now."

Buddy and Suzi thundered upstairs and returned a few moments later with their bathing suits on. Mary Anne couldn't help smiling. In his suit, Buddy turned out to be a skinny little boy with big, knobby knees, and Suzi was pudgy with a fat, round tummy.

"That was fast," said Mary Anne. "What did you do with your clothes?"

"Threw 'em on the floor," replied Buddy.

Mary Anne pointed up the stairs. "Back," she said. "Go back and pick them up. Put them on your bed – *neatly.*" She turned to Suzi. "Where are your clothes?"

"In my doll bed."

Again Mary Anne pointed upstairs.

After much grumbling, Buddy and Suzi returned. "Now what?" asked Buddy.

"Now," said Mary Anne, "Marnie and I take off our shoes, Marnie puts on her boots, we all put on our raincoats and rain hats, and then we go for a walk in the puddles."

"Barefoot?" asked Suzi incredulously.

"Almost," said Mary Anne. She had found a whole bunch of flip-flops – all sizes – in the closet, and she handed them around.

"Oh, boy!" cried Buddy.

So Mary Anne and the Barretts headed outdoors for a puddle walk. The day was wet but very warm. Mary Anne herded the kids down the drive and on to the pavement. "Jump in as many puddles as you can," she told Buddy and Suzi. "Try to make big splashes."

"Eee-*ii*!" shrieked Buddy, running towards a wide puddle. "Bonsai!" He leaped into it, sending out a spray of warm puddle water.

"He splashed me!" accused Suzi.

"Good," said Mary Anne. "That's the idea. You're wearing your bathing suit and your raincoat. Those clothes are *supposed* to get wet."

"Oh," said Suzi. Then, "Blam!" She jumped into the puddle with Buddy. She and Buddy ran down the side.

Mary Anne followed slowly with Marnie, who liked to get into a puddle and stay in it, patting her boots in the water and laughing. Between puddles, she stooped down to examine every worm she saw. She would poke them, smile at them, and then look up at Mary Anne and give her the ham face.

The puddle walk ended when Suzi threw a worm at Buddy, and Buddy said, "The puddle walk rule is, if you throw a worm, you have to eat it. So, here. Take a bite." He held the worm out to Suzi.

"No, no, no!" Suzi began to cry again.

"All right," said Mary Anne. "The puddle walk is over. It's time to go camping."

Back at the Barretts' house, the raincoats and bathing suits were hung up to dry, and everyone got dressed again. Then Mary Anne helped the kids make a "tent" by throwing some old blankets over a card table in the playroom. They added "rooms" to the tent by overturning the kitchen chairs, placing them by the table, and covering them with more blankets.

"Kristy and I used to make tents all the time," Mary Anne told me over the phone, "but this one was the biggest I've ever seen."

The Barrett kids loved the tent. Suzi and Buddy crawled around inside it, playing an imaginary game about camping and bears and spacemen. Marnie invented a game of her own, which involved peeking at Buddy, Suzi and Mary Anne from under the tent flaps.

When it was time for the picnic (orange juice and crackers), the kids wanted to eat in the tent. Just as they were finishing up, the phone rang.

"I'll get it!" shouted Buddy. "It's the space phone."

"Sorry," said Mary Anne, remembering that I'd said Mrs Barrett didn't want the kids to talk to their father. Besides, she had a feeling I might be calling.

Buddy scrambled out of the tent anyway, but Mary Anne was hot on his heels. She reached the phone at the same time he did, and since she was taller, she answered it first.

Out of sheer frustration, Buddy gave her the Bizzer Sign.

"Hello," said Mary Anne. "Barrett residence. Can you hold on a sec?" She covered the receiver with her other hand. "Buddy, you are in trouble. Go to your room."

Buddy stuck his tongue out at Mary Anne and stomped upstairs.

"Hello?" Mary Anne said again.

"Hello," answered a man's voice. "Who's this?"

"This is Mary Anne Spier, the babysitter. Who's this?"

"This is Mr Barrett. May I speak to Buddy, please? Or Suzi?"

"I'm sorry, they're . . . they're at a friend's house," Mary Anne lied.

"Oh, *fine*," said Mr Barrett, and slammed down the phone.

Mary Anne felt afraid. What was wrong? Why didn't Mrs Barrett want Mr Barrett to talk to the children? Was Mr Barrett angry at Mary Anne now? Did he know she had lied?

Probably, Mary Anne decided.

There was a scene when Mrs Barrett came home. Buddy was mad because he'd been punished, and Mrs Barrett was mad both because Buddy had misbehaved and because Mr Barrett had phoned.

"He's only supposed to speak to the kids on alternating Tuesdays. That's part of the custody arrangement. This is the wrong Tuesday. He can't keep his own schedule straight," she said, fuming.

"And, Buddy, what is the *matter* with you? I get notes from your teacher; you give Mary Anne trouble. I don't have time for this, young man. I cannot be your mother and your father, run this household, look for a job, *and* straighten out the messes you get yourself into. It's too much to ask of anybody."

Buddy, standing at the top of the stairs, began to cry silently.

At the bottom of the stairs, Mrs Barrett did the same thing. Then she opened her arms and Buddy rushed into them. Mary Anne, who had already been paid, tiptoed out the front door.

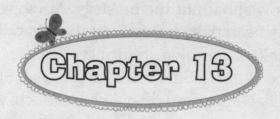

Chapter 13

The rain continued for several more days. Although it was dreary, I didn't mind it – much. It was kind of like the California rainy season. Meanwhile, my mom was in a great mood. She went around smiling and whistling. The house became more organized. Three straight days went by in which I didn't once have to tell her to change her clothes.

She talked to Mr Spier on the phone almost every evening.

The Barrett kids, on the other hand, were being driven mad by the rain. Four days after Mary Anne sat for them, I sat for them. There had not been a drop of sunshine since the puddle walk. It was a Saturday. The weather forecast was for rain ending before noon, followed by cloudy skies.

By the time Mrs Barrett had been gone for an hour, I was as zooey as the Barretts were. They didn't want to do *any*thing, not even take a puddle walk or make a tent.

"How about putting on a play?" I suggested.

"No!" said Buddy.

"Making our own comic book?"

"Too hard," Suzi said grumpily. She was scrunched down in a corner of the couch, wearing a sundress, her mother's high heels, and a plastic mixing bowl as a hat.

"Well, what *do* you want to do?" I asked.

"I don't know. What do you want to do?" replied Buddy.

"Get a big piece of paper and make a mural?"

"Nah," said Buddy.

"Pretend we're spacemen?"

"Nah," said Suzi, peering at me from under the bowl.

We were back where we had started.

I sighed and looked out of the window. That was when I noticed that the rain had stopped – actually stopped. The sky was still heavy and grey, the ground was soaking wet, but it *wasn't raining*.

"Hey! Look at that!" I exclaimed. "The rain stopped. Let's play outside."

"Yay!" cried Buddy and Suzi.

There was a mad scramble for the back door.

"Whoa! Just a sec," I said. "Buddy, you're dressed to go out – as soon as you put your boots on – but Suzi, you aren't. And neither is Marnie. It's chilly out there today. You can go on outdoors, Buddy, and we'll be there in a little while."

Suzi immediately began to whine. "I want to go *out*, Dawn. No fair. *Buddy's* going out."

"You're going to go, too," I told her as I led her upstairs, Marnie in my arms. "But you need to put on trousers, a shirt, a sweater, and boots. Marnie, too. You guys'll freeze in those dresses."

I helped Suzi change first. From the window of the girls' bedroom, I could see Buddy in the front garden. He had put his boots on, as well as his Mets jacket, and was tossing a baseball around.

Then I set Marnie on the changing table. It took a bit longer to dress her, because she needed a clean nappy, and as soon as I changed it, she wet it again, so we had to go through the whole process a second time.

At last the girls were ready. They struggled into their rain boots and we went out of the door to the garage.

"Get the mitt," I told Suzi. "Buddy's in the front yard with the baseball. Maybe he'll toss you a few."

"OK!" She found the mitt and she and Marnie

and I ran into the yard. There was the ball, but no Buddy.

"He must have gone around back," I said. I picked up the ball, and we looked in the yard behind the house.

No Buddy.

"Buddy?" I called. "Buddy? Bud-*dee*!"

I listened for his answer, but the only sounds were the rain dripping off the trees and, in the distance, a car horn.

"Bud-*deeee*!" Suzi yelled.

"Maybe he's hiding," I suggested. "Buddy! If you want to play hide-and-seek, come out so we can choose 'it'."

Nothing.

I began to get angry. "Buddy, if you don't come out right now, you're going to be in very big trouble. I'm not kidding."

"I bet he's over at the Pikes'," said Suzi. "I bet he wanted to play with Nicky."

"I hope so," I replied. "But even if he is, he's in trouble. He's always supposed to let me know where he's going to be."

I put Marnie in her pushchair and she and Suzi and I walked down the street to the Pikes'. Suzi rang their bell. Mrs Pike answered the door.

"Hi, Dawn," she said. "Hi, Suzi, Marnie. What

a nice surprise." She reached out to tickle Marnie.

"Hi," I replied. "Listen, is Buddy here? I'm babysitting and he went outside a little while ago. Now I can't find him. I thought he might be playing with Nicky."

Mrs Pike frowned. "No, he's not here. At least I don't think so. Let me get Nicky, though. Maybe he knows where Buddy is." Mrs Pike leaned inside and called Nicky. A few moments later, he appeared in the doorway.

"Sweetie," said his mother, "Dawn's looking for Buddy. Do you know where he is? Did he come over today?"

"No," said Nicky. "I was hoping he would because I want to show him my new walkie-talkies."

"But he hasn't come by?" Mrs Pike asked again.

Nicky shook his head.

"Did he call you?" I asked.

"Nope."

"Well," I said, forcing a smile, "I'm sure he's around somewhere. I'll go back to the Barretts' and look some more."

"Try calling the Murphys. And the Spencers," suggested Mrs Pike. "And let me know if you don't find him in about half an hour."

"OK," I replied.

I pushed Marnie to the Barretts' house so fast that Suzi had to run to keep up with me.

There's no reason to panic, I kept telling myself. This is a big neighbourhood with lots of kids. Buddy could be anywhere.

Even so, my heart was pounding and I was beginning to feel nervous. Buddy was my responsibility. I was supposed to know where he was.

At the Barretts', I plopped Marnie in her playpen, much to her dismay, and Suzi and I checked the house and the yard thoroughly. Unless he was in a very clever hiding place, Buddy was definitely not at his home.

I called the Murphys and the Spencers. No one had seen Buddy. But Mr Murphy gave me the names and numbers of four other neighbours. I called every one of them.

Not a trace of Buddy.

Feeling panicky, I phoned Mrs Pike. "I've looked everywhere and called all the neighbours!" I cried breathlessly. "I can't find Buddy."

"Keep calm," said Mrs Pike. "Call the Spencers and the Murphys again while I phone some other neighbours. We'll spread out and search for him. I'm sure he'll turn up."

Twenty minutes later, a big group of people, including Mr and Mrs Pike and seven little Pikes (Jordan was at his piano lesson), were gathered in front of the Barretts'. Mrs Pike took charge.

"Everyone spread out and look for Buddy," she instructed us. "Go in pairs or in groups of three. Younger children go with an adult. Come back here if you have anything to report. I'll stay with Dawn by the phone in case Buddy calls."

The neighbours dispersed excitedly. Mrs Pike and I went inside and I put Marnie down for a nap. When she was settled, I ran into the kitchen, where Mrs Pike was fixing Suzi a sandwich.

"Have you called Mrs Barrett?" Mrs Pike asked me.

"I can't reach her," I replied. "She drove to Greenvale to shop. Maybe her phone is off."

Greenvale is a historic town about thirty miles from Stoneybrook. The main street has been fixed up to look the way it did two hundred years ago, and it's lined with quaint shops. The town is sort of a tourist trap, but it's a lot of fun.

"Oh, Greenvale," said Mrs Pike. "Did she say anything about eating lunch there? We could try calling the restaurants."

I shook my head. "She just said she was going shopping."

"Oh, well, I don't suppose calling her would do much good anyway. She'd just panic and come home."

I wandered anxiously to the front door and back into the kitchen. "Why hasn't someone found him by now?" I asked. "How far could he have gone?"

"I don't know, sweetie," said Mrs Pike, "but he'll turn up."

"What if he's hurt?" I cried suddenly. "What if he climbed a tree and fell out or got hit by a car or something? Maybe he's lying somewhere unconscious and that's why he hasn't come home."

"Try not to think that way," said Mrs Pike. She eased me into a kitchen chair across the table from Suzi and set a glass of milk in front of me.

I couldn't drink it. "Once I read about a little girl who fell in a septic tank," I said. "Buddy could have fallen down one. Or—"

At that moment the phone rang. I leaped for it. "Hello. Barrett residence. Buddy, is that—"

"Hello?" said a woman's voice. "This is *The Stoneybrook News*. Would you be interested in a subscription? We offer a special discount to—"

"No, thanks," I interrupted her. "Sorry." I hung up the phone. "Newspaper subscription," I told Mrs Pike.

She looked disappointed.

"Dawn?" said Suzi. "Someone's at the door."

Mrs Pike and I dashed to the front door, where we found Mr Murphy, Mr Prezzioso and Mallory Pike.

"Just checking in," said Mr Murphy. "No luck. The three of us walked all up and down High Street. Then we looked in the backyards along Slate Street."

A few minutes later Vanessa Pike, Mrs Prezzioso and Jenny checked in. They hadn't had any luck, either.

Just as they were leaving, Jordan Pike turned up. "Hi, Dawn," he said. "Hi, Mom. I got your note and I came over like you said to. What's going on? There are all these people outside."

"Honey, Buddy's missing. Everyone's out looking for him. You haven't seen him by any chance, have you?"

"Sure I have. And he's not missing," replied Jordan.

I could have jumped for joy. "Where is he? Where is he?" I cried.

"He's at his lesson."

"Lesson? What lesson?" I asked. Mrs Barrett was disorganized, but she wouldn't forget to tell me if one of the kids was supposed to go to a lesson – would she? "Suzi, come here for a sec," I called.

Suzi ran out of the kitchen and joined Jordan and Mrs Pike and me on the front porch. "Suzi, does Buddy take any kind of lessons – like piano lessons or art lessons?" I asked her.

She frowned. "No. . ."

"Are you sure?"

"No. . ."

"Honey, what makes you think Buddy is at a lesson?" Mrs Pike asked Jordan.

"Because at the same time Mrs Katz and Sandy picked me up for my piano lesson, I saw someone pick Buddy up. So I just thought—"

"You saw Buddy get in a car with someone this morning?" Mrs Pike exclaimed.

Jordan nodded.

Mrs Pike turned to me. She looked stricken. "I'm going to call the police," she said.

I followed her inside the house, feeling dazed.

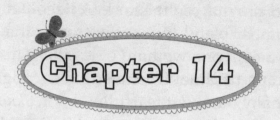

Chapter 14

After Mrs Pike called the police, everything started happening so quickly that the afternoon went by in a blur.

First Suzi began to cry – hard. So when Mallory came by the Barretts' again, her mother told her to take Suzi, Claire and Margo back to the Pikes' house for a nap. It would be quieter there, and they didn't need to be around when the police arrived.

Shortly after Mallory left, Mrs Spencer arrived, carrying a small red sneaker. It was rain-soaked and muddy. "I found this near the sewer on High Street," she reported. "It's not Buddy's, is it?"

I breathed a sigh of relief. "No, thank goodness. It's too small for him, and he was wearing boots."

The police arrived next. There were five of them. Two left as soon as they had a recent photo of Buddy. (I grabbed it off the coffee table in the Barretts' living room, frame and all.) Another one asked me questions, while the last two asked Jordan questions.

They were more interested in Jordan than in me.

Over and over, they asked him the same questions: What did the car look like? Did you see the number plate? Can you describe the driver? Was it a man or a woman?

Jordan became frustrated, then frightened, and finally burst out tearfully, "I don't *know*, OK? We live three houses away, and besides, I wasn't paying attention. I didn't think there was any reason to. Mrs Katz was backing down our drive and as we turned on to the street I saw the car pull up next to the kerb in front of the Barretts' house and I saw Buddy get in. That's *all*."

"It was a blue car?" asked one of the policemen.

"Yes."

"And you didn't notice the driver?"

"No."

"Did Buddy look scared as he got in the car? Did he look like he didn't want to go?"

"No, he was just opening the door and getting in."

"Did you recognize the car? Have you seen it around here before?"

"I don't know. It was just a car." A tear slipped down Jordan's cheek. He wiped it away with the back of his arm and glanced around, looking ashamed. Most of the neighbours had gathered, and Jordan was embarrassed to be seen crying.

Mr Pike put his arm across Jordan's shoulders. "Any more questions?" he asked the police.

"Just a couple," replied one. "Jordan, I know we've asked you this before, but are you positive you didn't see the driver? You can't even tell us whether it was a man or a woman?"

Jordan took a deep breath and let it out slowly. He was trying to control his temper. "I didn't see," he said after a moment. "I was looking at Buddy, not at the car or the driver."

"One last thing," said the policeman. "About what time was it that you saw Buddy get into the car?"

(I thought this was a dumb question because I'd already told him that Buddy had disappeared sometime between eleven and eleven-fifteen, but I guess they had to follow certain procedures.)

Jordan turned to Mrs Pike. "Mom, what time did Mrs Katz pick me up?"

"At eleven-fifteen, honey."

"Eleven-fifteen," Jordan told the policeman. "My piano lesson was at eleven-thirty."

The cop nodded his head and made a note on a pad of paper.

Meanwhile, I had finished answering the

144

questions the third policeman was asking. He wanted to know what Buddy was wearing, how old he was, where his mother was, whether anything unusual had happened during the morning – and a lot of stuff about his father. He especially wanted to know where Mr Barrett lived and what I knew about the divorce. He looked disappointed when I said I didn't know where Buddy's father lived, or anything about the divorce, but he was quite interested when I said that Mrs Barrett didn't like Mr Barrett to call the kids.

When he was finished talking to me, I sat down on the ground right where I'd been standing, bent my head down so that my hair fell around me, hiding me, and let the tears begin to fall. I cried and cried.

After a while I felt a hand on my back.

"Dawn?" said a gentle voice.

It was Mom. Someone must have called her. Probably Mrs Pike. I could tell she had sat down next to me. Without a word, I leaned over to her. She put her arms around me and held me for a long time.

When I felt better, I sat up. "I guess I ought to get back to work," I said, sniffling. "Marnie will be awake soon, and the police are trying to find out where Mr Barrett lives."

Mom patted my back. "You're a brave girl. I'm very proud of you."

"I wouldn't mind if you stuck around, though," I told her.

She smiled. "I plan to. The police have decided to organize a search of the neighbourhood, even though Jordan saw Buddy get in the car. Jeff and I are going to help out. We'll stay right around here."

"Thanks," I said. "Thanks a lot."

For the next hour, the police came and went. They searched the house for an address book or any clue to Mr Barrett, but didn't find much. Mrs Barrett seemed to have hidden away all information about her ex-husband. I even called Suzi to see if she knew where her daddy lived, but all she said was, "In his 'partment."

I took care of Marnie, who was up from her nap and hungry. Sometimes the police asked questions, sometimes they needed to use the phone. Under the direction of the cops, the searchers combed the neighbourhood. Six German shepherds joined in.

I fed Marnie, then brought her out on the front porch and let her toddle around the yard. I recited nursery rhymes to her. I sang songs. Marnie made the ham face.

146

"Silly girl," I said.

The phone rang.

I picked Marnie up and ran into the kitchen.

"Hello?" I said urgently.

"Hello?" said a small voice. "Dawn?"

"Buddy, is that *you*?" I cried.

"Yes, I—"

"Buddy, where are you? We're worried to death. Where *are* you?"

"In a gas station."

"A gas station? What? Where?" I didn't know what to ask next. "How did you get there? Whose car did you get into?"

"Dad's."

"Your father's?"

"Yeah, but I don't think I'm supposed to be with him. I knew you'd be worried, though, D—" The connection went bad. Buddy's voice faded away.

"BUDDY? BUDDY?" I shouted.

Very faintly, I could hear him saying, "Dawn? Hey, how does this thing work?" He must have been in a pay phone.

Just before the line went dead, he yelled, "We're on our way home, Dawn. OK? Dawn? We're on our w—"

"Buddy!" I shouted.

At that moment, the phone was grabbed out of my hand.

I screamed and whirled around.

It was one of the policemen. "It's Buddy, it's Buddy!" I babbled. "He's with his dad. He's at a gas station somewhere. He said they're on their way home."

The policeman, whose name was Detective Norton, looked puzzled. "There's no one on the line," he said. He hung up and got on the phone with the police station.

I began to indulge in a fantasy. The fantasy was that Mr Barrett would return, the police would see that Buddy was OK and would leave, the neighbours would do the same thing, and Mrs Barrett would come home and never know anything had gone wrong.

Unfortunately, Mrs Barrett showed up about fifteen minutes later. She came home to find the neighbourhood swarming with searchers (they hadn't been called off, despite the phone call), and two policemen having coffee in her kitchen.

She turned pale and dropped her shopping bags on the floor. "Dawn, what's going on?" she exclaimed.

I cleared my throat. "Well, Buddy disappeared this morning, and Jordan Pike saw him get into some car. So Mrs Pike called the police and everyone's searching."

"Oh, no." She sank into a chair.

"But Buddy called a little while ago. He's with his father. I don't know what's going on, but, anyway, he said he was on his way home. Oh, and Suzi's at the Pikes'. She's fine."

Mrs Barrett looked dazed.

"Are you all right, ma'am?" asked Detective Norton.

"Yes, fine, thanks," she said briskly. She put her hand to her forehead. "I'm just trying to think. . . I'm sure this isn't Ham's – that's Hamilton, my husband – I'm sure this isn't his weekend to see the kids. At least I don't think. . ." She got up and crossed the kitchen. By the phone was her engagement calendar. She flipped a few pages. "Oops," she said. "It *is* his weekend. I was mixed up. But I wonder why he only has Buddy, and why. . ." She trailed off in confusion.

Twenty minutes later, Mr Barrett still had not arrived.

"Ma'am, I don't mean to alarm you," Detective Norton began, "but has your divorce been a friendly one?"

"No, it hasn't," Mrs Barrett answered. "Why?"

"Because," replied the detective, "many of

the children missing today in this country are children of divorce. They've been taken by parents who want custody of them, but have not been granted custody."

"Oh, *no*," exclaimed Mrs Barrett firmly. "Ham and I have problems, and I know he feels he doesn't get to see the kids enough, but he'd never kidnap them."

"Are you sure? A parent will do desperate things for his children."

Mrs Barrett poured herself a cup of coffee. She stirred it thoughtfully. But before she said a word, we heard car doors slam, and the next thing we knew, Buddy burst into the kitchen, followed by a tall, sheepish-looking man.

Buddy ran to his mother and gave her a hug. Then he ran to me and gave me a hug. "I'm sorry I made you worry, Dawn," he said. "I'm starving. Do we have any cookies?"

I found cookies for Buddy while the police sat Mr Barrett down and began asking him questions furiously. Apparently, earlier in the week Mr Barrett had become angry when he'd realized that once again, Mrs Barrett had confused the dates and had forgotten that today was to be Mr Barrett's day with Buddy, Suzi and Marnie. He had decided to teach her a lesson. His plan was to come by on

Saturday, simply take the children, and wait for Mrs Barrett to figure out her mistake. So he drove over to the Barretts' house. There he found Buddy by himself in the front yard. At that moment, he decided that the easiest course of action would be just to take Buddy without bothering to look for the girls. So he did. He drove Buddy to an amusement park and took him out to lunch, but Buddy didn't seem to be enjoying himself. When he asked him what was wrong, Buddy said he was worried about me. He didn't think I knew where he was. That was when Mr Barrett realized that Mrs Barrett wasn't even home. Concerned about what a babysitter might do when she discovered that one of her charges was missing, he headed home immediately, stopping briefly at the gas station on the way. He'd tried to call before that, but had only got busy signals, and didn't even know Buddy had phoned until they were on the highway again. (Buddy had called while his father was in the men's room.)

The police gave Mr Barrett a warning, but that was all. However, they did strongly suggest that the Barretts talk to their lawyers about the custody arrangements. Just before I finally left, I told Mrs Barrett I would be back the next day.

I had something to tell her.

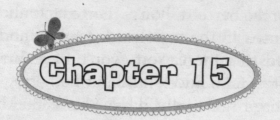

Chapter 15

Mrs Barrett and I were sitting on the Barretts' back porch. It wasn't Mr Barrett's day to spend time with Buddy, Suzi and Marnie, but Mrs Barrett had suggested that he take them – considering the mess she had caused the day before.

The house was quiet. I had never heard it so quiet. No running feet or yelling voices or crashing toys. Mrs Barrett had served us glasses of iced tea and had brought out a plate of cookies.

We both added sugar to our tea, stirred it, and took a sip.

"So, Dawn," said Mrs Barrett, "what is it you wanted to talk about?"

I put my iced tea down and drew in a deep breath. "Mrs Barrett," I said, "I really like Buddy and Suzi and Marnie, but I can't babysit for them anymore."

Mrs Barrett looked at me in dismay. "You *can't*? Why not?"

152

"Because of what happened yesterday."

"Mr Barrett? But we're going to straighten our problems out. We're going to talk to our lawyers just like the police suggested, and maybe a counsellor, too. You won't have any more problems with my ex-husband."

"That's not really what I meant," I replied. "The problem is . . ." How did I tell Mrs Barrett the problem was *her*? "The problem is that I've had a lot of trouble because of mistakes that . . . mistakes-you've-made," I said in a rush.

Mrs Barrett knitted her eyebrows. I couldn't blame her. After all, I was just a twelve-year-old kid, and I was telling her she was careless.

"I'm really sorry," I said, "but I can't be a good babysitter unless the parents give me a little help. I don't know your children as well as you do. I need you to tell me things about them – like whether they have allergies. And I have to know where you are while I'm in charge. If you're doing errands, that's one thing, but when you go somewhere in particular, I need to have the phone number."

"The right phone number," Mrs Barrett added thoughtfully, and I knew she was thinking about Hurley's Garage.

"Yes," I said. "But it's even more than that. I

need . . . I need some organization. And I can't do all your housework any more. And yesterday was very scary. And you know what else? Buddy and Suzi are starting to depend on me – a lot. Buddy comes to me with school problems now. Suzi calls me on the phone. Sometimes she doesn't really know what to say, but other times she's telling tales on Buddy or telling me about something that's gone wrong. I love Buddy and Suzi, Mrs Barrett. Marnie, too. But I think they should be going to you more. I mean, *you're* their mother. Not me."

Mrs Barrett didn't say anything. She just stared at me. She was looking as beautiful as usual – all cool and fresh, with her long, slim legs crossed in front of her. Mrs Barrett was gorgeous. She always looked so together. But her house didn't and her kids didn't. And I had decided that not only was babysitting for them too risky and too much work, it wasn't even good for the Barretts. I wasn't helping them. I was just allowing Mrs Barrett to go on being rushed and disorganized. As long as I was around to take care of things, then Mrs Barrett didn't have to take care of them herself.

Since Mrs Barrett wasn't saying anything, I stood up. "I'm sorry," I said. "That's why I can't sit for you any more. Your kids need *you*, not a babysitter. I talked this over with the Babysitters

154

Club, and they agree with me. The other members think I'm doing the right thing."

Mrs Barrett suddenly found her voice. "Oh, Dawn, please. Just a minute. Don't go. You're the best sitter I've ever found. The children *adore* you. They talk about you all the time. I think they'd be very hurt if you stopped sitting for them."

"Well, I'll still come visit them sometimes. And I'll see them in the neighbourhood when I'm babysitting at the Pikes' or the Prezziosos'."

"Couldn't we work something out?" Mrs Barrett asked.

"Like what?"

"How about if I asked you to come by ten or fifteen minutes earlier than I actually need you? That way we'd have time to talk before I leave. I could give you phone numbers and information. You could ask questions."

"Well. . ."

"And I'll try to keep the house in better shape."

"You know, Buddy and Suzi can help you with that," I told her. "They help me all the time. They're getting good at it."

"Maybe," Mrs Barrett went on, "if you did decide to sit for us, I could leave you specific chores to do sometimes and pay you extra for them. That seems fairer."

"Well. . ."

"Would you reconsider, Dawn?"

I thought for a moment. At last I said, "How about a trial? I'll babysit for you three more times and we'll see how things go."

"It's a deal," said Mrs Barrett. She stuck out her hand and we shook on it. Then we finished our iced tea and had a very nice time talking about Buddy and Suzi and Marnie.

At the next meeting of the Babysitters Club, I told my friends what had happened when I talked to Mrs Barrett. They thought I'd been very brave to have the talk in the first place.

"And so," I said as I finished up the story, "I think it was all right to agree to sit for them again. After all, it's just for a trial period."

"I think it was OK, too," said Kristy. "It was reasonable. And we don't want to give the Babysitters Club a bad name by being unfair. It was good that you compromised."

Lately Kristy almost always agreed with me. Not when she didn't really mean it, of course. But she *used* to disagree with me on everything, just so she could pick a fight.

"How are the Barrett kids doing anyway?" asked Mary Anne. "I mean since Saturday."

"They're fine," I said. "Marnie never really

knew anything was wrong, of course. And Suzi spent most of that afternoon with Mallory Pike. Mallory is really good with little kids."

"I guess because of all her brothers and sisters," said Stacey.

"She'll make a good babysitter," added Claudia.

"Maybe one day the Babysitters Club will be a huge organization," I said dreamily, "and Mallory will be part of it." I smiled at the thought. "Anyway, Buddy's OK, too. A little confused, I guess, but his parents have explained to him that although they do have some problems, they're trying to work them out."

"The thought of parents kidnapping their own children is scary," said Claudia.

"Yeah," said Kristy. "I wonder if my dad would ever do that to my brothers and me. Or what if he just took David Michael – and we never saw him again? How awful." Kristy shivered.

I did, too. If my father kidnapped me, would I want to go back to California now? I wasn't sure. Although if he did kidnap me, I guess we couldn't go back to California. We would have to go somewhere where no one would think to look for us. Like Alaska. I definitely did not want to do that. Anyway, Connecticut isn't so bad when you get used to it.

I looked around at the members of the Babysitters Club – my friends. We were sprawled all over Claudia's room. Mary Anne and I were lying side by side across her bed on our stomachs. Kristy was slumped thoughtfully in the director's chair, and Stacey and Claudia were sitting on the floor. All of us, except for Stacey, were eating candy gummi bears that Claudia had stashed in a pencil case in her desk drawer.

The phone rang.

I picked it up while Mary Anne poised her pen over the appointment book. "Hello, Babysitters Club," I said.

"Hi, Dawn. It's me, Buddy."

"Hi, Buddy, " I replied. I raised my eyebrows at the girls as if to say, "What now?"

"You know what happened in school today? All I did was drop my pencil on Steve's desk and my teacher goes, 'OK, Buddy, no recess for you.'"

A thousand questions popped into my mind like, Did you *throw* your pencil on Steve's desk or did you really just drop it? How many times had you already dropped your pencil on Steve's desk? But instead I asked, "Buddy, is your mom home?"

"Yes."

"I think you should tell *her* about this. She'll help you decide what to do. She's good at that."

"Not as good as you."

"Give her a try, Buddy," I said. "But you know what you can tell me? You can tell me if anything funny happened at school today."

"Well," said Buddy slowly. "Ashley Vaughn's lunch fell out of the window."

"That's pretty funny," I told him, laughing. "OK, I've got to get off the phone now." (Kristy was shooting looks at me because we're not supposed to have personal phone conversations during the meetings.) "Talk to your mother tonight, Buddy, and tomorrow when I babysit you can tell me what she said."

"All right," he agreed.

We hung up.

The members of the Babysitters Club discussed business for a few minutes. Then Kristy cleared her throat and got to her feet.

Something was about to happen. I could tell. Mary Anne and I sat up, and Stacey and Claudia stopped fooling around with the gummi bears and looked at Kristy.

"You guys," Kristy began, "I've been thinking over this problem of what to do

159

about the club after I move. I know we have all summer before that happens, but I can't help worrying about it. And I've come to a decision."

I turned to Mary Anne in horror. Suddenly I was sure – *sure* – that Kristy was going to break up the club. I could feel tears pricking at my eyes. I looked down so that no one would see me cry.

"My decision is to raise our club fees."

My head snapped up in surprise. "Raise our fees? Why?" I asked.

"Because the only solution I can think of is to pay someone to drive me to and from the club meetings. Not a taxi driver – that's much too expensive – but someone who'd like to earn a little money. It would be an easy job, and for someone young who's just learned to drive—"

"Charlie!" cried Mary Anne suddenly. Charlie is Kristy's older brother. "Charlie will be able to drive then, won't he? Oh, Kristy, that's a wonderful idea! He'll be dying for excuses to use the car."

"But do you mind paying for it out of our fees?" she asked us. "It seems like a club expense to me, since I *am* the president and I have to be at the meetings, but—"

"No, it's the perfect solution!" I agreed.

"Perfect!" echoed Stacey and Claudia.

Whew. What a load off everybody's minds.

Two days later, a "surprise" visitor came to one of our club meetings. It was my brother, Jeff, and the only person he was a real surprise to was Mary Anne. The rest of us had asked him to come over with the new camera my dad had sent him. Kristy and I had had an idea. Mary Anne was almost finished redecorating her room. (She even had a new rug, a new bedspread, and newly painted walls, courtesy of her father, who was becoming less and less tight with pennies and dollars.) But she didn't have the one thing she'd been talking about ever since she started the project – a framed photo of the members of the club.

The day Jeff came over, Kristy, Claudia, Stacey and I went to the meeting very carefully dressed. (We knew Mary Anne would look nice, because she always does.) When we told Mary Anne why Jeff was there, she burst into tears. But she dried them quickly.

"OK, everybody, why don't you pose on the bed," suggested Jeff.

So we did. Claudia, Stacey, and I kneeled against the wall and Kristy and Mary Anne sat in front of us.

"Smile!" said Jeff.

We grinned. Mary Anne grinned the hardest.
Click, click went the camera.

And the five members of the Babysitters Club were captured for ever.

Be part of something special!

The Babysitters Club

Don't miss **The Babysitters Club ⑥** :

Kristy's Big Day

Nothing can ruin Kristy's big day . . . as long as the BSC sticks together!

Mom was leading a large group of people into the back garden – all six Fieldings, plus Watson, Andrew and Karen.

Courage, I told myself.

Everyone exchanged hellos.

Karen took Andrew's hand and led him to the table where Claudia's art stuff was set out. "I'm going to draw a big, ugly picture of Morbidda Destiny," I could hear her say.

But the Fieldings hadn't moved an inch. A baby was huddled in his mother's arms with his face buried in her neck. A girl about Grace's age was holding Mr Fielding's hand solemnly.

And a little boy and girl were clutching their father around his legs, their faces also buried.

Watson leaned over and whispered to me, "They're all very shy."

Now this is the sort of thing that kills me about Watson. Duh. Of course they were shy. Any fool could see that.

Mrs Fielding spoke quietly to her children. "This is where you're going to play today. Andrew and Karen are here. See?" She pointed to the table where Andrew and Karen were colouring and giggling.

I knelt down to child level. "I'm Kristy. We're going to have lots of fun," I said. "There are swings and games and friends to play with."

The oldest child (Katherine?) bit her lip and gripped her mother's hand more tightly.

"Do you like dogs?" I tried. "We've got old Louie—"

"A dog, Daddy?" whimpered the little boy.

Oops, bad idea, I thought.

Mrs Fielding tried to untwine the baby from around her neck. "This is Tony," she said. "I think I'll just put him in the playpen."

She did so, with Katherine trailing behind, holding on to her mother's jean skirt.

Tony's face slowly crumbled. He sat on his bottom with his arms in the air and his lower lip trembling. His eyes filled with tears. Then, very slowly, he opened his mouth and let out a shrill, "Wahh!!"

Mary Anne turned pale.

Mrs Fielding looked flustered. "I think – well, we'll just leave him there. He'll stop crying after a while. Now, this is Katherine."

"And this," said Mr. Fielding, indicating the little boy attached to his left leg, "is Patrick. And this is Maura." (Little girl attached to right leg.)

Katherine, Patrick and Maura made no moves to leave their parents.

I glanced at Mom. Mom glanced at Watson. They talked to each other with their eyes. Finally, Watson clapped his hands together and said heartily, "Are the adults ready to go?"

"We have a lot to do today," added my mother.

Mr Fielding pulled Patrick and Maura off his legs.

Mrs Fielding got herself out of Katherine's grip. "We'll see you this afternoon," she said to her children.

The adults walked around to the front of the house and piled into their cars.

Katherine, Patrick, Maura, Tony, Beth and Peter all began to cry. Andrew took stock of the situation and began to cry, too.

Something else us babysitters didn't count on: seven crying children.

"Quick, put on the rest of the name tags and divide into groups," I said.

We did. Stacey and Dawn had no criers, Mary Anne and I had two criers each, and every kid in Claudia's group was crying.

But nobody panicked. Mary Anne put Tony in Beth's Walk-a-Tot and Beth in her pushchair, and walked Beth around the yard as Aunt Theo had suggested.

I talked quietly to Andrew and he stopped crying right away. Then I took my group off to a corner of the yard, pulled Katherine onto my lap, and began to read Green Eggs and Ham.

Claudia had a tougher job, but she did what I did, and led her three criers to a different corner, sat down and began reading Where the Sidewalk Ends. Soon every one of our criers had become a giggler. And Mary Anne's criers were quiet.

When I finished reading Green Eggs and Ham, I looked around the yard and took a fast head count. Stacey was sitting at one of the picnic tables with Luke, Ashley and Emma. They were making woven place mats out of construction paper.

Nearby, Dawn was playing Monkey in the Middle with David Michael, Berk and Karen.

Claudia and I were reading to our groups, and Mary Anne had successfully put both babies in the playpen and was tickling their feet.

Good. Fourteen happy children. The first crisis was over.

Don't miss a meeting!